the Double Cousins
AND THE MYSTERY OF
THE CAMP PROWLER

the Double Cousins
AND THE MYSTERY OF
THE CAMP PROWLER

MIRIAM JONES BRADLEY

AMBASSADOR INTERNATIONAL
GREENVILLE, SOUTH CAROLINA & BELFAST, NORTHERN IRELAND
www.ambassador-international.com

The Double Cousins
And the Mystery of the Camp Prowler

ISBN: 978-1-62020-756-7
eISBN: 978-1-62020-759-8
Library of Congress Control Number: 2020935900

Cover Design and Page Layout by Hannah Nichols
Ebook Conversion by Anna Riebe Raats

AMBASSADOR INTERNATIONAL
Emerald House
411 University Ridge, Suite B14
Greenville, SC 29601, USA
www.ambassador-international.com

AMBASSADOR BOOKS
The Mount
2 Woodstock Link
Belfast, BT6 8DD, Northern Ireland, UK

The colophon is a trademark of Ambassador

Dedication

This book is dedicated to the pastors and workers who have served at Black Hills Baptist Camp over the past fifty-one years. Generations of children have been blessed by your servant hearts.

Author's Note

As a child, my favorite event of the year was church camp—just like the Double Cousins. My dad was the director and my mother the cook, and I waited all year for camp to roll around again. Then, as a young nurse, I returned to camp in Wyoming as a camp nurse. I learned something—I still loved camp just as much as I did when I was young.

Fast forward several years and I was made aware of a camp in the Black Hills of South Dakota that had run for almost thirty years at that point. For the next eight years, I went every summer and was a counselor and/or camp nurse at Black Hills Baptist Camp at Camp Mallo in Four Corners, Wyoming. So, when I realized that my first Double Cousins book was destined to be a series, camp was the very next place I thought of setting a book.

But here we are, and the "camp mystery" is number six in the series. What happened? It was a simple matter of the timeline. Since the series started at the end of one summer and would run through the next summer, the camp mystery needed to wait its turn. Hard truth.

So, finally, I get to finish a book I started twelve years ago during NaNoWriMo 2007, before any of the books were published. But what happened during that time was that the series became more of a historical fiction series, and there was no real area history in my story. In addition, it was kind of short and needed some more excitement. So, I started researching the area around the camp; and truly, my wonderful nieces, nephews, and sister informed me of the true event that became the basis of the historic part of this story.

The stagecoach robbery is based on true fact. I have no evidence, though, that anyone ever found jewelry hidden somewhere up there, like in my story. The characters are not based on any one person but are a conglomerate of the many pastors, pastor's wives, and other adults who gave up a week of work to help at camp. Gilly is certainly based on our dear Iris Two Cookies who does make sure no one takes more than two cookies. She has been coming to this camp since she was a child in 4H, and no, I don't know how many years ago that was. Gilly's childhood was completely made up by me.

For fifty-one years now, this camp has consistently provided a quality camp for children throughout the Northern Great Plains. I hope they know just how much they are loved by those of us who were blessed by their servant leadership and how much we appreciate what they do year after year.

Once again, I want to thank those who have helped me with this book. First, all of the campers who inspired me, especially my nieces and nephews. Secondly, my sister, Cheryl, and my nieces and nephews who were helpful in reminding me of camp details that I had forgotten. In addition, Jan Bennett, Cindy Jones, and Jessica Cook, who were beta readers and proofreaders. A huge thank-you to JhaRee Miller for the fantastic map of the camp! It will bring the story alive for those who haven't been there. And, finally, to my husband, Bruce, who continues to put commas in places that need them and helps me draw out some of the most humorous moments in the book.

JOHNSON-RAWSON FAMILY TREE

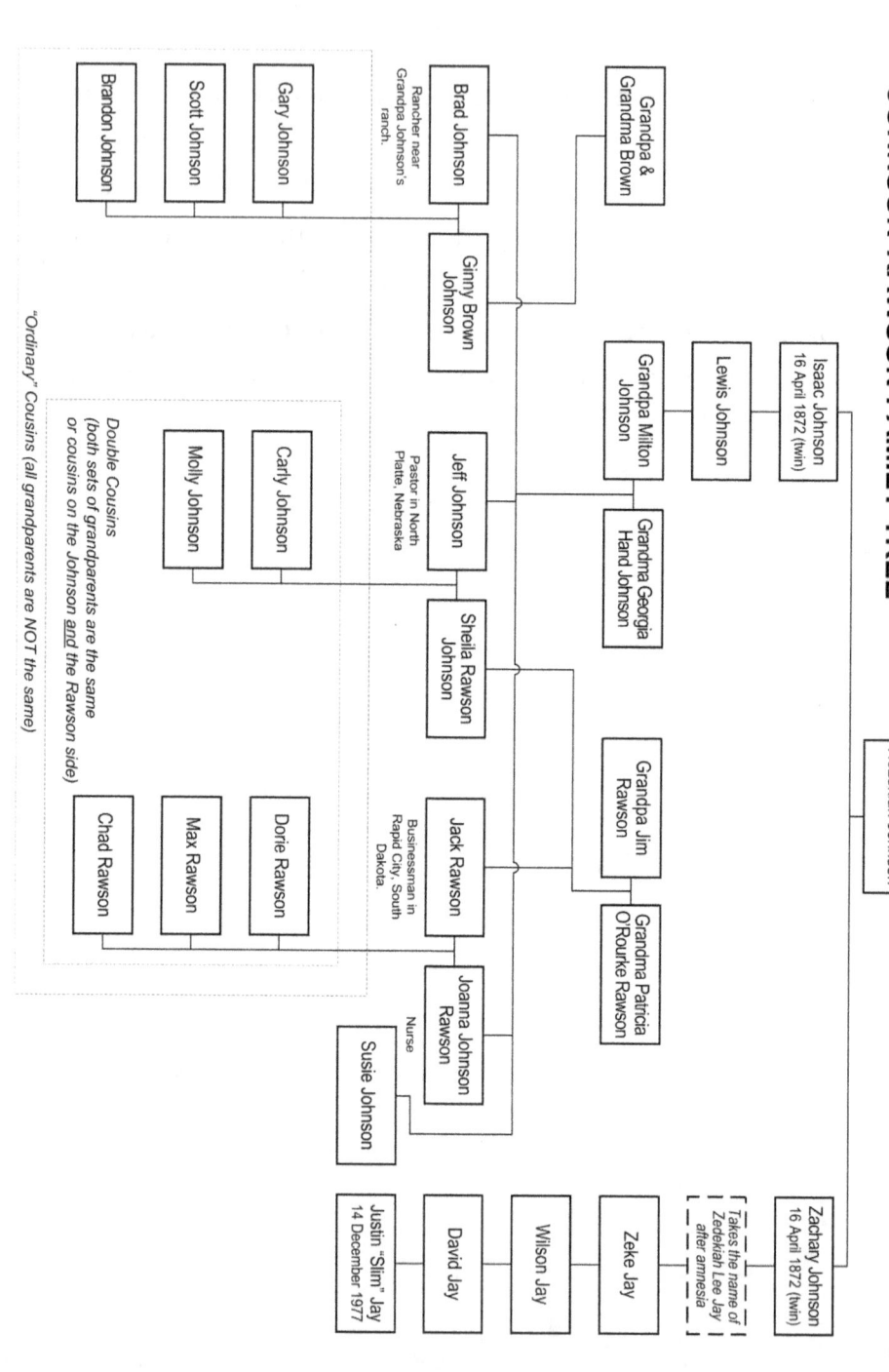

Hezekiah Johnson

Isaac Johnson
16 April 1872 (twin)

Zachary Johnson
16 April 1872 (twin)

Takes the name of
Zedekiah Lee Jay
after amnesia

Zeke Jay

Wilson Jay

David Jay

Justin "Slim" Jay
14 December 1977

Lewis Johnson

Grandpa Milton Johnson

Grandma Georgia Hand Johnson

Grandpa & Grandma Brown

Brad Johnson
Rancher near Grandpa Johnson's ranch.

Ginny Brown Johnson

Gary Johnson

Scott Johnson

Brandon Johnson

Jeff Johnson
Pastor in North Platte, Nebraska

Carly Johnson

Molly Johnson

Sheila Rawson Johnson

Grandpa Jim Rawson

Grandma Patricia O'Rourke Rawson

Jack Rawson
Businessman in Rapid City, South Dakota

Dorie Rawson

Max Rawson

Chad Rawson

Joanna Johnson Rawson
Nurse

Susie Johnson

Double Cousins
(both sets of grandparents are the same
or cousins on the Johnson and the Rawson side)

"Ordinary" Cousins (all grandparents are NOT the same)

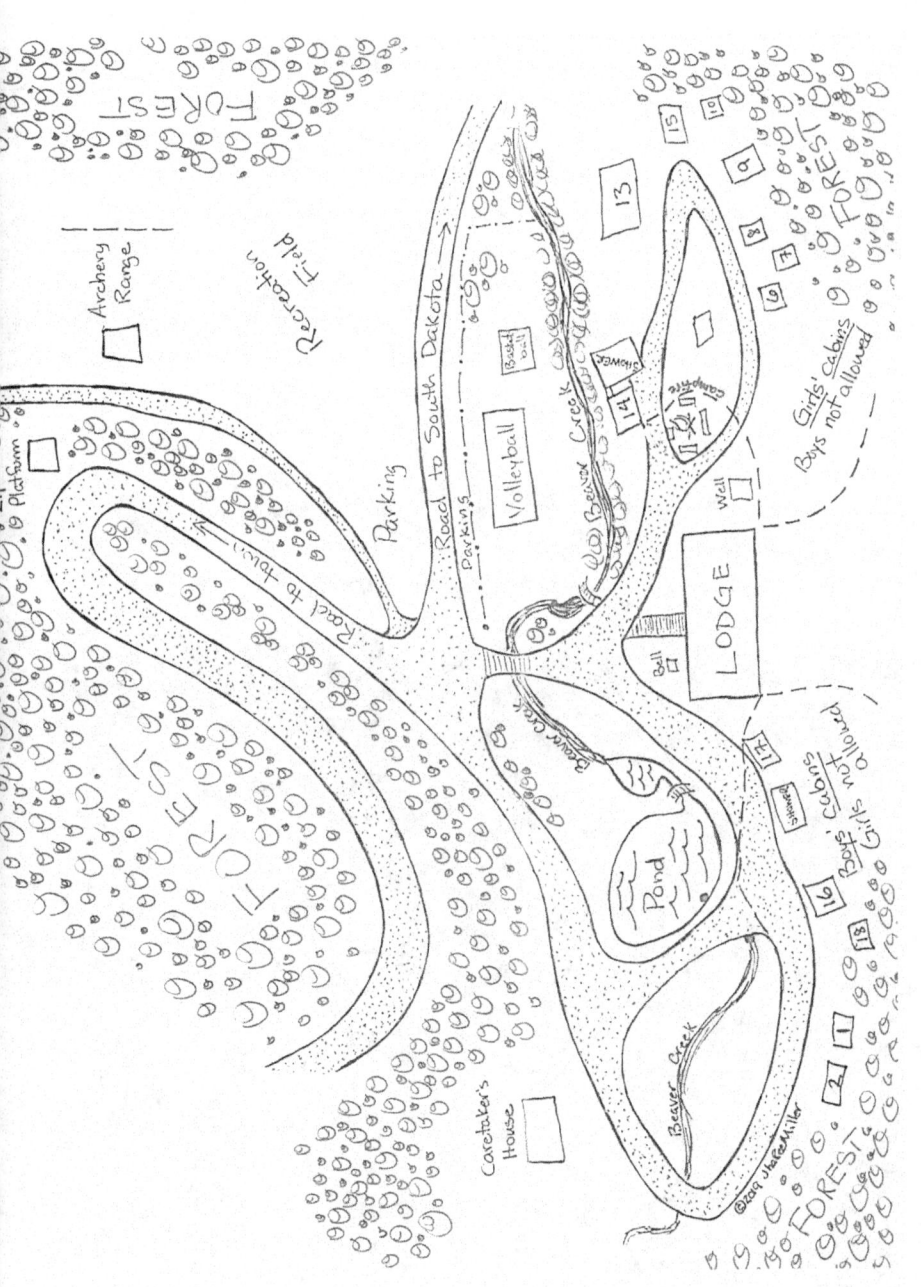

CHAPTER 1

July 1971

"Cookie! You in there?" Lily leaned on the wood counter at the service window between the kitchen and the camp lodge's dining area. She clutched an ice cream bucket filled to the brim with cookies and tapped the floor with her saddle oxfords.

"Just a minute!" The faint voice drifted out from the walk-in refrigerator. Ten-year-old Lily's red hair bounced as her head swung to the left toward the propped open door. As she watched, out popped the head, followed by the bent shoulders, and finally the rest of a very tall man. When he straightened to his full height of six feet eight inches, Lily giggled. *He looks like the rubber toy, Gumby, that Mike got for his birthday.*

"What's so funny, Lily, my Gilly?" Cookie hooked his hands through the belt of his white pants and smiled down at the girl on the other side of the service window.

"You reminded me of my brother's toy when you came out of the fridge all bent over like that." She shoved the bucket toward him. "I brought you some cookies, Cookie!" She bowed. "I made them myself. They're oatmeal raisin—your favorite."

13

"You're right; they are my favorite. I've never met a better oatmeal raisin cookie than the ones you make. Thank you! It saves us a lot of time and money for people to bring cookies for dessert. Say!" Cookie pointed a long bony finger at her. "I need you!"

Lily's mouth dropped open. "For what?"

"When you're too old to be a camper, why don't you come back here and help me in the kitchen? Then, when I retire, you can take my place."

Lily got a knot in her stomach. "That won't be for a long time, will it? I mean, the part where you retire?"

Cookie threw his head back and laughed heartily. "I hope not, Gilly. Lord willing, I'll be here for many more years."

"Good! Me, too." Lily blew Cookie a kiss, turned, and ran across the room. "See you later, Cookie. I have to take my stuff to the cabin."

Present Day

"Miss Gilly, I have some cookies for you." Eleven-year-old Carly Johnson, her dark hair pulled back in a braid, rushed across the dining hall toward the service window. She plunked the ice cream bucket filled with cookies on the counter. "I brought your favorite oatmeal raisin cookies from the recipe you gave me last year."

"Miss Gilly," as everyone called the cook, leaned on the counter, opened the lid, and took a deep breath. "Oh, those spices get me every time." She smiled at Carly and pushed a wisp of graying red hair behind her ear. "So, the cousins are back this year, huh?"

Carly laughed. "Yep, the same as every year since I was born. You know we always come. Why, Miss Gilly, you've known all of us since we were born, haven't you?"

Miss Gilly nodded. "I guess so. And I've known your parents since they were young, too. Pastor Jeff used to sit right in here when he was a kid and eat cookies. Me and your family, we go way back." Gilly smiled. "Why, I remember when those two Rawson kids first noticed the Johnson siblings. The next thing I knew, there were two weddings, and now we have double cousins at camp."

Carly giggled. "Daddy says we should thank God for this camp because without it, we might not be who we are."

Gilly nodded. "So, did the double cousins have a good year?"

Carly leaned across the counter, so Miss Gilly could hear her better. The huge room echoed with the voices of excited children. "This has been the craziest year ever! Last August, when we went to Grandpa Johnson's for a visit, he gave us a mystery to solve, and we've had nothing but one mystery after another all year. We've solved five already." She grinned. "Mom said we better not even think of finding one here." Carly threw her hands up in the air. "But we never look for them. They just happen."

"What kind of mysteries?" Gilly leaned on the counter, settling in for a long visit.

"Well, first we found what happened to the missing watch and discovered who Slim was. Then we found out more about Zach's story." Carly counted on her fingers. "Then we helped save Mr. Crosby's store and figured out the mystery of the Rushmore treasure."

Gilly held her hand up. "Whoa, girl. That's a lot of information." She pointed across the room. "Who's that young man with your aunt Susie?"

Carly turned and looked. "That's Slim. I was telling you about him. He's our fourth cousin."

"Looks like he might be something else before long, if I know anything about anything," Gilly muttered. "Are you all campers this year?"

"This is Molly's first year, so she's really nervous." Carly waved toward her younger sister seated in a chair by the door into the lodge. "Max and Brandon are campers, and Dorie will help with the crafts and watch the little kids, since she isn't a camper until next week. Mrs. Hammond's bringing her three. Chad's eight, but he's only going into third grade, so he can't be a camper yet."

Gilly lifted her eyebrows. "Wonder what he and Jeremy Hammond will get up to?"

Carly giggled. "No kidding! What about you, Miss Gilly? How long have you been coming to camp?"

"Oh, girlie, practically since the Great Flood." Gilly put her hands on her hips. "Actually, I was eight the first time I came here. That would make it fifty-one years."

Fifty one! "You've come every year?" Carly asked.

"All but one, I think. When I got too old to be a camper, but not old enough to be a counselor, I came and helped in the kitchen. After all, I *had* promised him I would . . . "

"Promised who?" Carly asked.

"Carly," Molly called across the room. "Come on, we need to get our cabin assignment."

"I'm sorry, Miss Gilly," Carly said. "We'll have to talk later. I have to go take my stuff to the cabin."

"You go ahead, honey." Gilly shook her head. "The more things change, the more it's all the same."

Chad Rawson was trapped between his brother, Max, and their cousin Brandon in the van's back seat. He poked his elbows into the two eleven-year-olds' sides. "Scoot over. You're squishing me." They shifted maybe a quarter of an inch, then stuck their elbows out so Chad had even less room.

"Dad, Max and Brandon are squishing me on purpose."

Mr. Rawson, in the driver's seat, glanced back in the mirror. "Boys, stop it. It's not much further. Hang in there, Chad." Pastor Byrd sat in the passenger seat, and the three Martin brothers rode in the middle.

Chad twisted to look over his shoulder. *Yep, Mom and the girls are still following us with the minivan.* Chad wrinkled up his nose. *They're eating our dust. Sure glad we're in front.*

"There's the cemetery; we *are* almost there!" Chad pointed out the window as they passed the little cemetery. Dust billowed out from under their van and tickled his nose as they drove slowly down the dry gravel road.

Max jabbed Chad in the ribs again and pointed back toward the cemetery. "Remember, Squirt, that's where the bad kids are sent. They get to spend the night with the dead people." Brandon and Max snickered.

Kevin Martin jerked around in his seat to look at Max. "You're kidding!"

Chad glared at Max. *Kevin's the only one here who hasn't been to camp before.* "It's just a joke, Kevin."

"Right." Chad's dad glanced into the rearview mirror again. "Don't let them scare you, Kevin. That's the 'new kid at camp' joke. Even if you did get sent there, you could easily walk back."

Kevin didn't look convinced.

"I suppose if some of the boys aren't quiet at bedtime, we could make them hike up here," Pastor Byrd said. "In the dark."

"Pastor Byrd is the camp director," Max explained to Kevin. "He makes sure we keep the rules. He may even make you grind wheat in the kitchen for Miss Gilly if you break too many."

"How do I know the rules?" Kevin asked. "What if I don't know them? I made myself several maps so I know where to go, but what if I don't know the rules? I know the part about not going on the girl's side of camp, and I know you have to eat all the food you take." He slid down in his seat.

Kevin's brother, Bill, put his arm over his shoulder. "Don't worry, Kev. You stay with us, and you'll be okay. Besides, they tell you the rules first thing."

Pastor Byrd turned in his seat. "Kevin, let me tell you how the camp got started. I'm pretty sure the rest of the boys don't know all this."

Chad leaned forward to hear better just as Max and Brandon did, also. *Great, I'm still squished.*

"Over fifty years ago, several small, independent churches in the Great Plains area met together for fellowship," Pastor Byrd said. "Soon, they realized a mutual problem—their children needed a good camp. So, the churches decided to do something about it. They rented this campground for two weeks in July, and the first week had Junior Camp for grades fourth through seventh and the second Senior Camp for grades eighth through twelfth."

"Is it still the same group of churches now?" Kevin asked.

Pastor Byrd nodded. "Mostly. Of course, churches have changes; and sometimes, the church is unable to come. Other times, they may find another camp they prefer. And we have some new churches coming now. But our fellowship association has maintained this camp all these years."

"That's really cool," Max said.

"One of the wonderful things about it is that it's staffed by people from the churches," Chad's dad said. "I think that's important because the people who are here with the campers are also at home to encourage them afterward."

Pastor Byrd winked at Kevin. "Now if someone gives you a hard time about being new to camp, you can share the history with them."

Chad sat back in his seat and stared out the window. *Over fifty years. That's practically ancient history! Dad wasn't even born yet.*

Chad's heart raced as the vans wound their way down the steep hill into camp. He leaned forward to look out the side window, then sat as tall as he could to see out the front window, waiting for his first glimpse of the lodge. Even though Dad crept like a snail down the hill, the washboard road rattled the van until he thought his teeth would shake right out of his head. When they rounded the last curve, the entire camp unfolded before them in the valley below. Chad cheered.

The lodge sat on the far side of the valley, up against the hill. The stone building blended into the terrain, and the wide porch welcomed the campers. The valley was ringed by hills covered with dark evergreen trees, and it seemed to Chad they were entering another world. Chad's dad and Pastor Byrd rolled down the windows, and the fresh mountain air rushed into the van. Chad took a deep breath. *I love the smell of camp.*

A church bus and four RVs brought by some of the staff sat to one side of the big playing field. Children were everywhere: in the sand volleyball court, the basketball court, and even a few in the creek, which ran through the camp and fed the small pond where the campers fished. Several vehicles had parked by the lodge to unload, and children milled all over the yard, suitcases in hand and sleeping bags thrown over shoulders.

When the vans pulled to a stop at the lodge, the kids tumbled out. The adults climbed out a bit more slowly.

"Look," Brandon said, pointing toward the porch. "It's Cousin Slim and Aunt Susie!"

"If it isn't the rest of the cousins!" Slim said. He and Aunt Susie hurried down the steps. "We've been here only about ten minutes. We were just headed in to see where we're supposed to bunk." Slim winked at Max and Brandon. "You might have to put up with me."

"I hope so," Max said.

"I wish I could be in your cabin." Chad clung to Slim's arm.

"Your mom needs your help, Chad," his dad said. "Besides, didn't you tell me Jeremy Hammond will be here? You'll find lots to do."

Chad brightened. "Yeah. Me and Germy have lots of plans."

"Germy?" Chad's dad shook his head. "I'm not sure he'll like being called that."

Chad snickered. "Germy and me have nicknames for each other. Mine is Chadstick."

"Jeremy and I. It's Jeremy and I, not me and Jeremy." Dorie glared at Chad, and he glared right back.

"You aren't my teacher, and we're at camp, not school, anyway," Chad said.

"That's enough," their dad said. "Go get registered. I'll start unloading, so we can get this van out of the way. More vehicles are coming down the hill, and there's not much room here to unload. We don't want to block traffic through the camp."

Mr. Rawson opened the van's back door. "As soon as you're registered, come right back out, get your stuff, and take it to your cabin. Chad, you stay here and help me. You know what you and your mom need in your room."

Chad watched as the others hurried into the lodge. *Next year. Next year, I'll be a camper.*

When Max stepped through the door into the lodge, he shivered. *I bet it's ten degrees cooler in here.* The tables, lined up on the kitchen end of the lodge, awaited the campers, and chairs faced the other end where the group meetings were held. A keyboard and marimba were already set up by the podium, and a large curtain behind them blocked the view of the staff's rooms along the building's left side. The smell of baking lasagna made Max's stomach growl.

A line had already formed at the registration table, and Max spotted Carly and Molly right away, about halfway up the line. Pastor Hall sat behind the table, and Pastor Byrd hurried around to help. "I'll get the girls organized if you give me their lists," he said, a twinkle in his eye. "We'll get it done in half the time."

"Hi, Carly. Hi, Molly," Max said as the girls shifted over to Pastor Byrd's line.

Carly turned around. "Hi! We just got here."

"We thought we'd never make it," Brandon said. "I've been at Max's the past week. That's why I didn't ride with you guys."

"Then you would have had an eight-hour ride here to the corner of Wyoming," Carly said. "We left North Platte at six o'clock this morning."

Molly pushed Carly forward in line. "We slept until about eight in the car," Molly said. "It did make the trip go faster."

"All right, you Johnson boys. You're up. I suppose you have an opinion about what cabin you want." Pastor Hall didn't crack a smile. "Yes, sir," said Max. "We want Cabin Three."

As soon as Max mentioned the cabin number, Pastor Hall shook his head. "I'm sorry, Max. That cabin is out of commission. It's set up for an educational opportunity for 4H clubs this summer. Did you know it's the original cabin from when the camp was built?"

Max looked at Brandon. "Cabin Four?" Brandon asked. "That's second best."

"Okay, Cabin Four it is."

Even though Pastor Hall rarely smiled, the twitch of his lips gave him away. *He's not as stern as he tries to look.*

Once registered, the cousins met up outside on the broad front porch. "I'm glad we're in a cabin with Aunt Susie and Mommy," Molly said.

Carly picked up her sleeping bag and suitcase. "Me, too. With the five other girls already registered, we'll have a full cabin. But we get Cabin Seven. That's the one we wanted!"

"We're in Cabin Four with your dad and Slim," Max said. "We have five guys from our church, so we'll have room for three or four others. I hope I know some of them from last year."

"Hey, over there!"

Startled, Max looked across the yard. Chad stood by the pile of suitcases and sleeping bags, hands on his hips. "What are you waiting for? I've got better things to do than stand here and guard your stuff!"

"Guess we better rescue him," Brandon said.

Max laughed. "Poor Chad, left holding the bags." More campers burst out the door behind them. "We better hurry, too. We want to get good bunks before they're all gone."

A few hours later, the campers had settled in their cabins, and the lights were out. The girls in Cabin Seven were, for the most part, quiet, except for an occasional whisper. Every few minutes, loud voices or a burst of laughter came from the cabins on either side of them. Carly tried to lie still and fall asleep, but she couldn't relax. *I'm just too wound up; my insides feel jumpy.*

From her top bunk, she could see out the small window. The nearly full moon shone through the trees enough that she could even see the path to the bathroom. *It's so light out there.* As she stared out into the night, her mind flew back over the day, especially the part after they got to camp.

We have a good cabin. I like all the girls, and we worked well together to get stuff arranged in here. At five o'clock, the bell had rung, and they had lined up in front of the lodge to divide into teams and hear the rules before supper. *We have six teams this year with ten campers on each team.* Carly multiplied in her head. *That makes sixty campers. That's a good number.*

Carly kicked back the top of her sleeping bag. *I wish we could open the windows.* Carly smiled when she remembered how Molly and Cindy, a first-year camper from Sheridan, Wyoming, were convinced bats would fly in if they left the window open. Aunt Susie explained that the bats wouldn't come in unless it was lighter inside than outside; but the girls were still too scared, so they left the windows shut.

Team Five will be a good team. I'm glad Brandon is with me. We have some fast kids. She giggled when she remembered some of the games they had played last year.

"What's so funny?" Molly whispered.

"I was thinking about my team and some of the games from last year."

"Max is on my team—Team One," Molly said. "And that big boy, Jess. He sure doesn't act excited to be here. He was really mean to Kevin, that boy from Max's church."

Carly frowned. Jess had been there last year, and he had been in trouble a lot. When Jess got off the bus, Max's face had said it all. He wasn't thrilled that Jess was back.

"I feel kind of sorry for him," Carly whispered. "I don't think he's happy, no matter where he is."

"He's in Max's cabin," Molly whispered. "Maybe Slim can help him."

Carly thought back to a time when Slim wasn't happy with life either. *He hardly seems like the same guy Grandpa brought to the ranch last summer.* He had been silent, angry, and scared. But then, they discovered he was their distant cousin, and now they all loved him, especially Chad. The five mysteries the cousins had solved over the past year flew through her head. *Every time we get together, there's another mystery.* Carly grinned. The last thing her mom said to her before they left home was not to expect a mystery at camp.

From the cabin next door, laughter erupted again. "They're awfully loud over there," Molly whispered.

"I know. If Pastor Byrd hears about it, he'll say something tomorrow."

"You all settle down now; it's lights out," a male voice called from the path below their cabin. The noise from the other cabins stopped instantly. Carly froze in her bed and held her breath while she listened to hear if the man said anything else.

"Who's that?" Molly whispered.

"I don't recognize his voice, but it must be Pastor Byrd," Carly's mom said. "I'm glad you girls are quiet tonight. Good job!"

"I thought he wasn't coming around," Aunt Susie said. "Oh well, we better get some sleep. Remember, if any of you girls need the bathroom in the night, wake one of us up, and we'll walk down to the bathroom with you. That's the only thing I wish was different here. A bathroom in the cabin would be so nice." She yawned and turned over, causing the plastic cover on her bed to crackle. "That and the mattress covers. Good night, everyone."

"Good night," the girls whispered.

CHAPTER 2

Carly was startled out of a deep sleep when the big bell in front of the lodge rang at 7:15 Tuesday morning. Her nose was cold, and when she stuck an arm out, she pulled it back under the covers right away. *I guess it's a good thing we didn't open the windows last night.*

"Rise and shine," sang out Aunt Susie.

Carly peered over her covers. Molly sat on her bunk, rubbing her eyes. Jody and Trisha, sisters from North Dakota, shivered as they pulled on their jeans and sweatshirts. Leah and Margaret, second year campers from Colorado, were still buried under the covers, and Cindy sat on the edge of her bed.

Carly grabbed her clothes from the bottom of her bed and wiggled into them under the covers. "It's cold out there. I guess the best way to warm up is to get moving."

A few minutes later, Carly and Molly ran down the hill to the lodge where the campers lined up in front of the steps for flag-raising—girls on one side, boys on the other. Max and Brandon stood at the front of the boys' line with Jess.

"Hey, Carly," Max said. "Did you guys get any sleep last night?"

Carly's teeth chattered as she zipped up her hoodie. "I slept great once I got to sleep! Did Pastor Byrd come by and tell you to be quiet?"

"Yeah!" Brandon said. "At least, we figured it had to be him, but it didn't really sound like him."

"I don't think it was him," Jess said.

"Why not?" Molly asked.

"The guy I saw out the window looked taller than Pastor Byrd, that's all." Jess shrugged, hands in the pockets of his baggy pants.

"You saw him?" Carly asked.

"Just for a second. I didn't see him that well." Jess stomped in place. "Man, I could use some coffee. I can see my breath, it's so cold out here!"

The lodge door opened, and Pastor Byrd hurried down the steps. "Good morning, campers! How did you sleep last night?"

Several of the kids snickered. "Our cabin was the quiet one," Molly said. "Cabin Seven. You didn't hear anything coming from Cabin Seven, did you?"

"I didn't hear anything from any of them," Pastor Byrd said. "I was in the kitchen talking to my wife on the phone."

"Well, someone came around and told us to be quiet," Max said. "We all heard it."

Pastor Byrd gave them the thumbs-up. "Good! Sounds like someone was helping me out, huh? All right. Jess, do you want to ring the bell? Let's get this show on the road. I don't know about you, but the smell of breakfast is making me hungrier. Besides, Miss Gilly will be out here telling me we're late if we don't get moving."

Jess hurried to the huge bell in front of the porch and pulled on the rope. The strong, clear peal echoed across the valley announcing flag-raising and breakfast.

Chad sat on the end of a bench at the table closest to the kitchen door. He rubbed his eyes and yawned. Jeremy was still asleep in the room they shared with their mothers, Dorie, and Jeremy's four-year-old twin sisters, Corrie and Cassie. *They sure can talk. I thought they would never shut up so I could go to sleep last night.*

Chad let the grown-up conversations roll over him as he watched the activity in the kitchen. Miss Gilly always put out cold cereal every morning, along with pancakes or French toast. She stood at the open window and filled cereal bowls while talking to Pastor Hall, who had just poured himself a cup of coffee from the big silver pot by the window.

"I don't know who it was, but someone came into my kitchen last night." Something in her tone pulled Chad out of his drowsy state, and he looked up. Miss Gilly's face was red, and her lips tight. Even her hair looked redder than gray this morning. *Wow, she doesn't even look like Gilly. I've never seen her be anything but happy.*

"Whoever it was helped himself to bread, peanut butter, jelly, and cereal. He—or she—didn't even clean up the mess." Gilly glared at Pastor Hall as if he himself was the guilty party and slammed down a box of cereal. "Paul is checking the refrigerator right now, but I know they took candy, too. We hadn't opened any packages yet, and several have a candy bar or two missing. Every single one with peanuts in them has been opened."

"I'm sorry, Miss Gilly. I'll talk to the staff and see if I can discover anything. We'll get to the bottom of it. Don't worry."

"I hope so! It's hard enough preparing meals for all of these people without my supplies being pilfered."

Pastor Hall nodded. "You're right. I'll let you know what I find out."

Slim stood at the coffee station, stirring creamer into his coffee. "Good morning, Slim," Pastor Hall said. "How did your boys sleep?"

Chad got up and wandered over to the men and snuggled in beside Slim for a sideways hug.

Slim looked down at Chad, tousled his shock of red hair, and grinned. "Well, I was beginning to think we would have to take them on a hike to get the energy out of them; but when Pastor Byrd came by and hollered for them to be quiet, they settled down." Slim took a sip of coffee. "Then it was just dealing with the snoring and plastic on mattresses." He held up his paper cup and yawned. "The coffee helps."

Pastor Hall frowned. "It wasn't Pastor Byrd. He was on the phone in the kitchen for an hour while I visited with Gilly and her staff. You know," he dropped his voice, "she keeps some homemade snacks in the kitchen for the staff. Just make sure you ask first." He shook his head. "Someone was into her food last night, and she's pretty upset."

"Thanks for the tip," Slim said.

Chad tugged on Slim's hand. "Let's go out for the flag-raising."

"Great plan, Chad!" Pastor Hall said. "Let's all go. Slim, I'll check with Pastor Byrd about last night, and we'll ask around. It must have been one of the counselors."

Carly loved flag-raising. This morning, as usual, everyone had a sweatshirt or jacket on because mornings in the Black Hills tended to be brisk, sometimes dropping into the upper forties. The smell of pancakes cooking in the kitchen mixed with the smell of fresh pine trees wet with the morning dew. The counselors clutched coffee cups in their hands, the steaming liquid warming them. The sun peeked over the hill, and the campers shifted from one foot to another. Carly watched as two boys raised the United States and the Christian flags, her hand over her heart like everyone else. *Well, everyone but Jess.* Coach Joe put his hand on Jess's shoulder to remind him to take off his hat and stand at attention, but Jess shrugged his shoulder to push the man's hand off.

Uh-oh. Big mistake, Jess. Jess glared up at Coach Joe, who looked him right in the eye, not giving an inch. After a few seconds, Jess dropped his eyes to the ground and pulled his hat off. Mike, one of Max's friends from last year, nudged Max, but he took a step away and kept his eyes on the flag. Mike shifted from one foot to another and stared at Max.

Once the flags were in place, the campers and counselors said the Pledge of Allegiance to both flags, as well as to the Bible. Then Pastor Byrd pulled out a little Bible and read, "A friend loveth at all times." He looked at the campers. "Do you think that verse means you love your friends just when it's convenient?"

"No," the campers chorused.

"How about when it's beneficial to you?"

Some campers nodded; some said no. Others just shrugged.

Pastor Byrd smiled. "Of course, that's a trick question, and you know it. The verse clearly states that a friend loves at *all* times. Now, we can get confused about what love means. It doesn't mean we protect someone from the consequences of their actions because we are friends or that we have to agree with the wrong things they do. No, it means we love them, even when they are in trouble. Now, we hope we don't have any people this week with problems or consequences. But if we do, being a good friend means you don't gossip about it, point fingers, or ignore your friend. Instead, try and help them make better choices. Okay. Let's have a word of prayer, and we'll go inside and eat some of the good food Miss Gilly and her helpers have cooked up this morning."

When Carly climbed the steps to the lodge, Jess stood on the porch with Coach Joe and Pastor Byrd. His head was down and his shoulders slumped, but she could tell he was still mad. *Oh boy, he's going to have a long week.*

The cousins entered the lodge and went right to the food line. Carly picked up a tray and stepped up to the huge platter of pancakes. "Good morning, Miss Carly," said Pastor Sting, who helped serve meals. "How many pancakes do you want? One or two?"

"Just one," Carly said. "Thanks." She hurried on to the oranges, where she held her tray out to Mrs. Sting, who was serving them. "We love your marimba," Carly said. "It looks so fun."

Mrs. Sting beamed. "It's a lot of work to bring, but it gives so much joy, doesn't it?"

Carly nodded. "It sure does. See you at lunch." She hurried over to the pre-filled cereal bowls, grabbed a bowl of Cheerios, then looked across the dining room to find a place to sit. The tables were filling up, and the clamor of all the campers' chatter made it hard to think. From across the room, Carly spotted Chad. He stood on the bench and waved his arms.

"Looks like Chad wants us to sit with them," Max said.

"Ya think?" Carly laughed.

"There's room for all of us," Brandon said.

Carly, followed by Molly, carried her tray down the outside aisle, dodged around a boy who wasn't looking where he was going, and hurried to the table where Dorie, Chad, and Aunt Joanna sat.

Chad stuffed the last bit of his first pancake into his mouth and scooted down to make room for Max. "Did you have any sick kids last night?" Max asked his mom, the camp nurse.

"No. It was a good night. I guess everyone is still too excited to be homesick. I slept like a log. Here, have some milk." She pushed the gallon jug toward him, and he poured some for himself, then passed it to Carly.

"Listen up." Pastor Byrd's voice rose above the noisy din, and the campers fell silent. "When you're done, don't forget to take your tray up to Mr. Paul at the water tubs. And don't forget, you cannot throw food away. After tonight, if you take it, you eat it. Also, I would like to meet briefly with all the counselors and other adults by the piano. It won't take long, but I have a couple of questions I need to ask you."

"He's going to ask who told campers to be quiet and who stole the food," Chad said, his mouth full of pancake.

"Chad," his mom said. "Don't talk with your mouth full."

"What?" Max asked. "How do you know?"

Chad swallowed hard. "I heard Pastor Hall and Miss Gilly talking. Then Pastor Hall and Slim were talking, and he said he would get to the bottom of it." Chad swallowed the last of his milk and wiped his mouth on the back of his sleeve.

"Chad, use your napkin," his mother said.

"The bottom of what?" Carly put her fork down.

"Who stole Miss Gilly's food and who was telling kids to be quiet," Chad said. "Weren't you listening? I just said—"

"All right!" Max interrupted. "We know about someone telling the campers to be quiet, but what's this about missing food?"

"Miss Gilly said someone went in the kitchen last night. She said they ate a peanut butter and jelly sandwich and took all the candy. She said we can't have canteen because there isn't any candy left. She said . . . "

"Whoa! Chad! Are you sure about all of those details?" Mrs. Rawson looked her son in the eye.

"Yes," Chad insisted. "She said . . . well, I'm not sure it was *all* the candy. But she was definitely mad. She slammed the cereal around like she was in a boxing match."

"Sure, she did." Max shook his head. "Miss Gilly? She never gets mad. She might act grouchy sometimes, but she isn't really mad."

Chad pointed his fork at Max. "Ask Slim. He was there; he'll tell you."

"Well, don't let your imaginations run away with you," Mrs. Rawson said. "Chad, you start washing the tables as soon as they are empty. You know the tables will have sticky spots, so make sure you get them clean. I'm going to this meeting to find out what Pastor Byrd wants. And no," she said, looking around at the cousins, "I won't be running right back to report to the Johnson-Rawson Detective Agency. You're here to be campers, have fun, learn more about God, etc., etc., etc. You are not—and I repeat, *not*—here to make mysteries out of nothing!" With that, she turned, took her tray to Mr. Paul, and hurried to the piano, where the counselors were gathering.

Carly pushed her pancake around her tray. "She's right, you know. It's probably nothing. I bet one of the pastors got hungry in the night and made himself a sandwich and took some candy."

"Yeah," Max said. "And it was most likely a counselor trying to help Pastor Byrd last night when he went around and told everyone to be quiet."

"Hey! Don't throw your food on the floor!" Molly shouted.

Carly jumped at the sudden outburst, and the entire row of tables fell silent.

Molly rose half out of her seat and pointed her finger at a boy at the next table. "Someone has to clean that up, you know! Pick it up!" Molly glared at the boy until he reached down and picked up the offending pancake.

Carly tried to suppress the giggle bubbling up inside her. She glanced around the table. Everyone's eyes were huge, except for Molly's cousins. They were grinning. Molly didn't get mad often, but when she did—wowzers!

Dorie put a hand on Molly's shoulder and pushed a little to get her to sit down. She whispered just loud enough for their table to hear. "Uh, Molly, I'm not sure you want to be known as the food police your first year of camp."

Molly tossed her head. "I don't care. Picking up food off the floor is no fun. You guys know."

Carly nodded. "We've all taken our turn washing tables and picking up the scraps."

"Yeah," Chad said. "I'm glad you told him. I don't want to have to pick it up when I wipe tables!"

Jess hurried past the cousins' table with his tray. He snickered at Molly as he went by. "Mad Molly," he said. "Watch out for Mad Molly."

"Lay off, Jess," Max said.

Jess sauntered away like he hadn't even heard.

Max shook his head. "It's Jess I'm worried about. He's started off with a bang this year."

Carly nodded. "I know. Did you see what happened at flag-raising?"

"Yeah, and he was rude to Uncle Jeff last night when he told us to let him know if we needed to leave the cabin in the night. And one of the other kids from his church said something about Jess's dad, and I thought Jess was going to punch him. He would have," Max said, "but Slim grabbed him and told him to get on his own bed. I don't think he has a 'happy home life'—as our neighbor Mr. Crosby would say." Max shook his head. "I'm doing my best not to think the worst of him, but he isn't making it easy. It doesn't help that my friends from last year are mad at me when I stick up for him." Max pushed his cup in circles. "Last year, I would have been right there with them, saying bad stuff about Jess. But since Slim came—"

"Well, while you guys worry about Jess, I'll keep my ears open," Chad interrupted. "I'll let you know what I hear about the mystery."

Carly laughed. "Okay, Chad. You do that. We'll be too busy with class and recreation all day. We won't have time for any sleuthing." She looked at Max, who rolled his eyes.

Chad stood up, grabbed his tray, and stomped off. "You'll see. Germy and me'll find out what's going on, and we'll do it without you. You aren't the only ones who can solve mysteries."

"Jeremy and I," Dorie called after him.

CHAPTER 3

Carly was right. The day was packed with activity. First, they had to clean up their cabins, which Carly dreaded. *How one small room with six bunk beds can get so messy in one day is more than I can figure out.*

"It looks like our suitcases exploded in here." Leah stood in the narrow aisle between bunks, clothes, and open suitcases completely covering the floor around her. Sleeping bags were wadded up on the bunks, and clothes even hung from the rafters.

"We'll do better tomorrow," Aunt Susie said. "You'll see. I have a plan. For now, let's get the mess cleaned up as fast as we can. Someone write a note for the inspector, and in fifteen minutes, we will all gather down at the campfire ring for cabin devotions."

"I'll write the note," Leah said. "I brought stationery and stickers for decoration. Pastor Byrd likes it when we leave notes for him."

Carly dug in her suitcase and came up with a sandwich bag. "I have glass beads I got at the craft store that we can lay around the note on the bench. We have to make the note as fancy as we can so we win cabin inspection."

"Remember to put your folder and Bible on the porch," Carly's mom said. "You'll need them for classes this morning."

"I'll sweep." Margaret grabbed the broom.

"You'll have to wait until we find some floor before you can sweep." Aunt Susie helped Trisha lift her bag off the bed and place it in the space between beds. "We'll line up our suitcases, all facing the same direction."

"I've got the shoes." Carly sat on the floor, lining shoes up in rows under her bed.

After cabin devotions and the missionary lesson, Coach Joe gave a few instructions for morning recreation. "When I dismiss you, I want you to go out to the big field. Now, don't trample any pastors or small children on your way. Once there, find your team's number painted on the grass and sit in a circle. Okay! Do you have it?"

"Yes!" shouted the campers. Max pumped his fist in the air. *Finally, some action.*

"All right! Ready, set, go!"

With that, the campers made a mad dash for the door, and the lodge emptied out quickly.

Out at the field, the teams settled into their circles where they started the first game. "I knew it," Max said to Molly, who sat next to him in their team's circle. "It's the game where you learn your teammates' names."

"Start out by going around the circle with everyone telling their names." Coach Joe said. "Then, beginning with your team leader, each of you go around the circle and name each member. Once every team member has taken their turn, you are done. The first team to finish wins."

"This is dumb." Jess picked at pieces of grass he had torn out of the ground. "It's a baby game."

"Ice breakers are usually a little bit simple," Slim said. "And this is an ice breaker."

"What's that mean?" Kevin asked.

"An ice breaker is a game meant to 'break the ice' or help people relax and get to know each other." Slim pointed to Max. "You go first; then we'll continue clockwise around the circle."

Once everyone had stated their name, Slim started back around the circle and named each one. When he finished, the girl next to him took her turn. Most of the campers messed up on at least two names, and there was a lot of laughter. Jess ignored the process; but when his turn came, he sat up straight, pointed his finger at each person, and named them without a single mistake.

"How did you do that?" Max asked.

Jess shrugged and returned to his slouched position.

After the game ended, Coach Joe introduced the next game, a relay with hula-hoops. "Max," Slim said. "Can you go twice? We're short a team member."

"Who's gone?" Max looked around. He saw the answer before Slim could respond. Jess walked toward the lodge, Pastor Byrd's hand on his shoulder. "Is he all right?"

Slim nodded. "He's fine. He just has an appointment in the kitchen."

Max turned back to the game. *Uh-oh. I bet he has to grind wheat. Maybe Miss Gilly can set him straight.*

Jess's stomach churned as he followed Pastor Byrd through the doors into the kitchen. *This is so unfair. Everyone always treats me like there's something wrong with me. This place is dumb. I should have stayed home.* He glanced around the room, then dropped his eyes to the floor. *Man! All of those little kids are in here. They'll blab about me to the whole camp.* He glared at Chad, Max's little brother.

Chad stared back, his hand, holding a partially eaten cookie, frozen in place over his glass of milk. Jeremy, Corrie, Cassie, and Dorie sat at the table with him while Miss Gilly worked at the counter beside them.

Pastor Byrd cleared his throat. "Miss Gilly, I have a young man here who seems to want to grind wheat. Can you use his help?"

Conversation in the kitchen stopped, and the silence was thick. Jess felt heat move up his neck to his face, and a huge lump formed in his throat.

Jess glanced up. Miss Gilly peered over her glasses at him. He shoved his hands farther into his pockets and stiffened up. *What's she staring at?*

"Young man," Miss Gilly said, her voice firm but kind, "I'm sure you could make better use of your time; but if you really want to grind wheat, we'll let you. You can come right over here, and Mr. Paul will show you how to work this wheat grinder." She turned back to the bread dough she was forming into balls.

Mr. Paul, heavy beard and mustache twitching, led Jess over to the grinder and showed him how to turn the crank and pour more wheat into the reservoir and ended with a warning. "Don't stop until Miss Gilly tells you to. Otherwise . . . " He shook his head, turned, and walked away.

Otherwise what? Jess stared after the man for a minute. *Guess I'd rather not find out.* He started turning the handle.

Gilly rolled another piece of dough. "He may decide he wants to be the cook when he grows up. That's what I did. Of course, I never had to grind wheat, but you know the story, don't you?"

"I've heard it from other people but never directly from you," Pastor Byrd said.

"Well, now. That's where I got my name, you know. Cookie called me 'Lily, my Gilly,' and it stuck. He was the cook when I came here as a camper. I know, I know." Gilly chuckled.

Jess snapped his mouth shut and looked at the others. They stared at Gilly. "It seems like I'm too old to have come here for camp. Just you wait. You'll see how fast your life flies by. God says our life is like a vapor; it goes as fast as smoke drifting away. Anyway," she rambled on, "Cookie used to tease me that I needed to come and help him cook when I got too old to be a camper, and I did. I was too young to be a counselor, but I wanted to come to camp. It was the best week of my year."

She reached for another pan and put the full one on the stove with a towel over it. "My home wasn't the best place in the world."

She smiled at Jess. "My parents both worked, and they had their own problems. I went to church with a friend next door, and her family saved my life, I think. Every summer, for one week, I could get away from all the hard things at home and come where the people all loved the Lord. Why wouldn't I want to keep coming?" Her jaw jutted out. "And then, I liked working in the kitchen so much, I kept coming back to help Cookie. When he had to stop, I agreed to be the cook. He taught me everything I know about cooking. He's the one who made up the menu we have used for years. So, Mr. Jess," she said, "you better watch it, or you could end up the next cook at this camp." She threw her head back and laughed—a loud, boisterous noise that made everyone else in the room laugh, too.

Jess took a deep breath and smiled. *Maybe this Miss Gilly isn't so bad, after all.*

"Miss Gilly," Pastor Byrd said, "that's the best story I've heard in a long time. I think I'll use it in counselor meeting tonight. They need to hear stories about how camp changes lives."

Gilly nodded her head. "Speaking of counselor meetings, did you learn who raided my food?"

"No," he said. "I have a couple more ideas, though. I'll talk to you about it later." He glanced at the children finishing their snack. "I see Miss Gilly continues the tradition of spoiling the non-campers around here." He grinned. "Believe it or not, I was once one of those children tearing around the camp. I remember Cookie, too. He started this tradition of morning cookie break. He's also the original cookie guard. He made up the rule of taking only two cookies." He turned to Miss Gilly. "Where is he now?"

Gilly shook her head. "He's in a nursing home. He has Alzheimer's and wanders in the night. They were concerned he would get outside and get lost if they kept him at home. I stopped to see him Sunday before I came to the camp. I think he recognized me; but his attention would wander, and I'd have to tell him who I was again." She wiped her eyes on her apron. "He showed me that article from when he was a kid. You know, the one he kept framed here in the kitchen?" Gilly looked at Pastor Byrd, and he nodded. "He told me over and over about finding the jewelry from that stagecoach robbery."

Jess stopped turning the handle. *Stagecoach robbery?* Mr. Paul cleared his throat, and Jess darted a look at the man, then began grinding again.

"Stagecoach robbery?" Chad jumped out of his chair. "I never heard about no stagecoach robbery."

Pastor Byrd grinned. "I'll see if Dorie can take you kids over to Cabin Three. A lady from the historical society is giving each team a tour of the cabin. I'm sure she will share information from that event, too." He turned back to Gilly. "I'm sure sorry to hear about Cookie. One of these days, though, he will get to Heaven, and his memory will be perfect again."

"I'm forgetful enough." Gilly washed her hands at the sink. "I'm kind of looking forward to Heaven myself."

Max followed Molly into Cabin Three and blinked. The cabin was dim and gloomy after being outside and silent, except for the shuffling of the campers. He glanced around the room. *It sure is different from last year when we stayed in here.* First off, the bunks didn't look like much more than wood pallets built into the room. No springs. Just a wood pallet with a mat. *I'm glad we don't have to sleep on those.* The walls were lined with old maps, pictures, and articles. A lady about Grandma Johnson's age stood at one end of the room and beamed at the group as they found a place to stand against the walls.

"Come in." She nodded to Slim. "Please shut the door, too. It's hot outside, and we want to keep the cool air inside as long as possible."

Max's eyes took everything in as she spoke. "Good morning. My name is Judy Clark. I am from the historical society, and we wanted to share a bit of the history of Camp Mallo and the surrounding area with you. This cabin is the only original one left from when the camp was built. It was actually used by several families before it was moved here and the Mallo family used it until the camp was built."

"This cabin, as you can see, had quite primitive bunks for the first campers. Not nearly as nice as what you have now, is it?"

"No," the campers chorused.

Mrs. Clark smiled. "I think you'll like this next part. There used to be a stagecoach line that came very near here back in the 1800s. In fact, it was the site of a famous robbery in 1878—the Canyon Springs Stage Robbery. We have articles on the walls to describe more about that event, but I'll be happy to tell you a little more about it."

A shock ran up Max's spine, and a collective gasp came from around him. *A stagecoach robbery? Here? Why wasn't he ever told about this before?*

"This stagecoach robbery involved the armored stage named the *Monitor*. It was quite a special stagecoach built for the Homestake Mine to carry bullion shipments. It was equipped with several added security measures, like loopholes for guns and a treasure box bolted to the floor."

"Wow!" Molly said. "It sounds pretty safe."

The lady nodded. "The Homestake Mine believed so, but they didn't take any chances. They had armed men inside and a man who rode shotgun next to the driver."

"What happened?" Max asked.

"Well, one day in 1878, a gang rode into the station and put the station attendant in the granary. When the stagecoach arrived, they started shooting. One of the stagecoach guards ran for help, while the robbers dragged the stagecoach into the woods to work on the treasure box."

Max held his breath. There wasn't a sound in the room as they waited for Mrs. Clark to continue.

She shook her head. "In the end, they got away with over twenty-seven thousand dollars-worth of gold, jewelry, and money. That was a huge amount of money back then."

Max whistled.

"Did they catch them?" Kevin asked.

"Yes, eventually. And they recovered about sixty percent of the loot, but there were some gold bars that were never recovered."

The room erupted with whispers and chatter.

Max turned and looked at the wall behind him. An article caught his eye. The headline read, "Local Boys Find Jewelry Thought to Be From Canyon Springs Robbery." He pointed to the article. "What's this about?" he asked Mrs. Clark.

"Well, back in the mid-1900s, a couple of boys were exploring the woods above the camp, and they found some jewelry, which turned out to be from the robbery," she said. "A lot of people have explored this area since because many believe more of the loot is still buried out there somewhere."

Molly grabbed Max's arm. "Wowee-pizowwie!"

Max shoved his hand through his hair. *This is incredible! But what happened to the rest of the loot?*

June 1947

"I'm sure glad we can hike today." Carl Sherwood, twelve years old, trudged up the hill behind his best friend, George Benson. "It's been a couple of weeks since we've had a chance. I thought my dad would never stop finding more chores for me."

George stopped and leaned on the hiking stick he'd carved from a branch. He pointed below them. "Here's our favorite view."

Carl looked over the valley to the camp below. Camp Mallo had been there now for several years. He sighed. "Sure wish I could go to camp sometime, but my dad says we're too busy for that."

"Me, too. Most days, I spend all day at the store helping my dad."

The boys hiked on up the hill, Carl taking the lead. "I'm sure this is better, anyway. No one to tell us what to do and when.

My mom sent us some ham sandwiches and boiled eggs, and we've got our blankets so we can stay all night."

A crow flew overhead, cawing so loudly that he set off a cacophony of sound from other birds. "I guess that's the welcome committee," George said. "C'mon. Let's get to our hideout and set up camp; then we can explore some more."

Thirty minutes later, the boys were settled in the cave they'd discovered the summer before. It was cool and dry on this warm June afternoon. Carl pulled out the ham sandwiches his mom had sent and handed one to George. The boys sat on the ground, leaned against the wall, and ate their lunch. George handed Carl an apple. "My mom sent one for you, too."

A flash of lightning, followed immediately by a crack of thunder, made both boys jump.

"Wowee!" Carl hurried to the cave door just as the sky opened and a downpour obscured the view. "Well, I guess we won't be exploring out there for a while."

George looked around the dim area. "I brought my dad's brightest flashlight." He dug through his bag until he found it. "We can explore in here! Maybe we'll find those gold bars the stagecoach robbers buried!"

Carl laughed. "Not much chance of that." He reached into his bag and pulled out his flashlight. "But I'm with you on exploring. Let's see what is here."

Half an hour later, the boys had explored back as far as they could go in the cave. They came to two paths at one point and first took the right one until it dead-ended. They then backtracked and went down the left branch. Other than some animal bones, they didn't find anything interesting. Finally, the cave narrowed and ended with a nine-inch opening in the back wall.

Carl shone his light back into the crevice. "Looks like the end of the road for us. We won't fit in there." A flash caught his attention as he stared into the opening. "There's something shiny back there!"

"Here, let me try." George reached his arm in and felt around. "Sure hope there aren't snakes back here."

Carl shuddered. "That would be bad, sure enough."

"Hey, I got something." George pulled his hand out and held it under the light.

"Well, I'll be!" Carl whispered. In George's hand sat a brooch and matching earrings like Carl's mom wore when she dressed up. Only these were shinier than anything she had! Even covered in dirt, they still sparkled when the flashlight shone on the clear and green stones.

"Do you think those are real diamonds and emeralds?" George asked.

"I don't know." Carl shook his head. "They sure look fancier than any I've ever seen. But how did they get here? And why?"

"Beats me," George said. "Here, you take them. I want to see if there's anything else in there." George pointed his light into the crevice again. "There's something back there. Looks like some cloth." He reached in again and pulled out the remnants of a small, velvet jewel bag. It was filthy and half-gone. "It's been chewed up pretty good," George said.

"Sure has," Carl said. "I bet critters scattered the other jewels all over the place. If there were more."

George grabbed Carl's arm. "Do you suppose these could be from the stagecoach robbery?"

Carl nodded. "That's what I'm thinking. We've got to get these down the mountain to town and show them to our parents. They'll know what to do!" Carl looked around the back of the cave. "Maybe the gold is here, after all! And we discovered it!"

CHAPTER 4

At lunch, talk swirled around the afternoon activities. "I don't know why we have to have a rest time," Brandon said. "I'm not tired at all, and it makes me more restless to lie in bed for half an hour. I'd rather play basketball."

"Yeah, what do they think we are—babies?" Jess said. He took a big bite of his hamburger with the homemade bun. "Did you guys know Miss Gilly was a camper here when she was a kid?"

"No way!" Max said.

"Yep, then she came to help the other cook when she was too old for camp."

"That's cool," Carly said. "But what does that have to do with rest time?"

"Huh? Oh, the bun reminded me. I was in the kitchen helping Miss Gilly this morning, and she told us about it."

"Why were you in the kitchen?" Brandon asked.

"He was a bad boy," called Peter from the next table down. "He's always a bad boy. If there's trouble, Jess is involved somehow. You can count on it, like the sun comes up in the morning."

"Shut up, Peter," Jess said.

"That's enough." Carly's dad gave both boys a stern look.

Brandon put his head down and took a bite of his hamburger. He looked out of the corner of his eye at Max, who ate like it was the only thing in the world to do. Brandon glanced across the table at Carly and raised his eyebrows. The awkward silence stretched out like a muggy summer afternoon.

"I'm saying all my Bible verses from last year to Aunt Susie during rest time," Carly burst out.

"Why?" Brandon jumped into the conversation.

"Because you get points for quoting any of the verses you learned last year. You have to say them before the memory session on Tuesday, so this is my last chance." Carly's eyes twinkled. "I want to win this year! I came close last year; but the girl who won had said her verses from the year before, and that's how she beat me. So, I decided to try it this year."

"How many verses is that?" Molly asked.

"I said all six sections with eight verses in each, so that's forty-eight verses."

Brandon whistled. "That's a lot. Maybe I'll work on the verses for this year during rest time. It's better than lying there with nothing to do. I'll whiz through a few verses each day."

"Don't forget you have to start over each day," Max said.

"Oh, I forgot." Brandon whacked his forehead. "I hate that rule. It's dumb."

"No, it's not," Carly said. They want us to *really* learn the verses, not just remember them long enough to say them once. After repeating the verses several days last year, I barely had to review them for this year. It does work."

Jess stood up and grabbed his tray. "I won't win. I can't memorize. I hate memory time. It's the stupidest thing at camp. An hour of trying to cram words into my brain. Bo-o-o-ring!"

"I bet you would be good at it if you tried." Molly smiled at Jess. "You remembered our names the best at recreation this morning."

"What do you know?" Jess sneered at Molly. "You're just a little kid."

Pastor Jeff looked Jess in the eye. "She might be a little kid, but wisdom often comes in small packages. Don't disregard the small ones."

"Whatever." Jess stalked off to deliver his tray to Mr. Mike.

Brandon looked across the table. Max's face was beet red, and his fists clenched in front of him on the table. He started to rise from his seat. Molly grabbed his arm. "It's okay, Max. Leave him alone. It won't help for you to get mad at him. Besides, you'll get in trouble, too. You don't need that."

Max slouched back into his seat and looked at Molly, then Brandon. "It makes me furious when he picks on people."

Max stood with his back to Cabin Thirteen. Beside him were his teammates and the members of Team Five. He glanced down the row at Brandon and Carly and lifted his eyebrows. Brandon shrugged. *I wonder what game we are going to play now? This is new.*

Coach Joe set a plastic tote in front of them. "Today, teams One and Five will battle it out. Have you ever heard of Capture the Flag?"

"Awesome," Jess said. "Wish we played that every day."

"I always get captured right away." Molly slouched back against the wall.

Max could hardly stand still.

Coach put his hand in the air. "This isn't just your average game of Capture the Flag, though. This is Capture the Flag with a twist." He jerked the top off the bin and pulled out an airsoft gun.

A cheer went up from the teams. *WOW. Airsoft guns. They're just as good as playing paint ball but better 'cause Mom won't get upset about the paint on my clothes.* Max grinned at Brandon and Carly. "Watch out, cousins. Your team is about to go down!"

"Fat chance," Brandon said.

"No kidding," Peter chimed in. "We'll beat you so fast, you won't even know what hit you."

"Watch and see," Jess shouted.

Five minutes later, after Coach had shown them how to safely use the airsoft guns and explained the rules of the game, Team Five stood across the field; the flags were in their place; and Team One remained against the cabin. Every camper held an airsoft gun, loaded with little pellets. Max bounced in place, like a boxer waiting for the match. "Okay," Coach said. "When I wave this flag, you can go. Don't forget your defense as well as offense. I'll give you a couple of minutes to come up with a plan; then we'll start."

"I'll take defense," Jess said. "Why don't you lead the offense, Max?"

"I'll be on defense with Jess," Molly said. "At least, until I'm hit."

"I'm fast," Kevin said. "If you tell me what to do, I could help with offense."

Max nodded. "Good idea, Kevin. You are small enough and fast enough that if we clear the way, you might slip in and get the flag."

The other team members divided themselves up, and they came up with a basic plan just as Coach called, "Ready, set, go!"

The defense team tore off across the field with the offensive players scattered behind them. The next few moments were a frenzy. Max took out a couple of girls from the other team pretty quickly, but he didn't get a chance at Brandon or Carly. They were hanging back.

Within ten minutes, most of the players were captured and waiting in the "prison area." The prisoners shouted suggestions and cheered on their team members. It was down to Jess, Kevin, Max, and Molly on their team. The other team had only three: Carly, Peter, and a girl named Melissa. Molly stood by their flag, her airsoft gun ready. Melissa guarded Team Five's flag.

"Max, take Peter. I'll get Carly," Jess said. "Then we can gang up on Melissa and distract her, so Kevin can go in after the flag."

It didn't quite go as planned because Peter took out Molly. She threw her hands in the air and ran over to the prison area. Kevin raced in to defend the flag, but Peter was there first. Just as Peter reached for the flag, though, Max and Jess rushed him, and he ended up being taken out by both boys. As Peter stomped toward the prison area, he passed Max. "Guess you're taking orders now from Jess, huh? You'll be just like him before long."

Stunned, Max froze in place. "Max, watch out," Molly called. Max dodged to the right, barely escaping a shot from Carly. Kevin came from behind and took Carly out. Within moments, the game was over. Melissa was no match for the three boys left on Team One.

Jess slapped Max on the back. "We did it!"

Team One ran to the middle of the field for a post-win huddle. Jess grinned at Molly. "Guess you didn't get out first this time, did you, Mad Molly?"

Max cheered with the rest of them, but there was a knot the size of a fist in his stomach.

Am I going to lose all of my friends because I'm trying to help Jess?

"I'm doing crafts," Molly said. "I want to make one of those copper pictures. I've wanted to do the one of the puppy ever since I can remember. What about you, Carly?"

The campers were gathered in the lodge for canteen and to hear the options for free-time activities.

"I think I'll fish today." Carly counted on her fingers. "Tomorrow, I can go on the hike. Thursday, I'll do crafts; and Friday, I'll either do the zipline or archery."

"It's the zipline for me today. I love it," Max said. "One of the other days, I'll do the climbing wall."

"I'm doing the zipline today," Brandon said. "I wish I could go on it every day, but it's a popular activity, so you can do it only one day, maybe two."

"I went last year." Carly shrugged. "It was all right. But I've never tried archery, and I hear Pastor Byrd gives you candy if you hit the balloons."

"What are you going to do, Jess?" Molly asked.

"Fish. I love to fish. My dad and I like to fish when he's off for the weekend."

Just then, Chad, Jeremy, the twins, and Dorie hurried through the lodge from their room, each carrying a towel. Their flip flops slapped the cement floor as they marched across the room.

"Looks like they're headed to the creek," Carly said. "I wish we could do that! It's hot enough today. It would sure cool us off."

"Another good reason to do crafts." Molly fanned herself with her folder." I hope it cools off for tomorrow. I want to go on the hike."

"Maybe all of us could go on the hike tomorrow," Jess said. "If you want to, that is." His voice faded away.

"Oh, let's." Molly clapped her hands. "It will be more fun if we all go together."

Molly caught the look on Max's face. *Uh-oh, I bet he doesn't want Jess to go.* She bit her lip.

"Sounds good to me," Brandon said. "I love the hike. The best part is when we get to the cliff and can see down over the whole camp."

"I'm in," Carly said.

Jess beamed.

Chad stomped through the creek below the foot bridge. It was so cold, his feet ached. *I'll get used to it.* He stomped harder, and water flew in every direction. "I wonder how high I can make the splashes reach," he said. He stomped in a shallow spot, but the water went more sideways than up.

"Hey, Chadstick!" Jeremy said. "You almost splashed me!"

"Sorry." Chad moved up the creek a little and stomped in a small pool. The water went both out and up. *So, that's how it works.*

Jeremy bent over downstream from him and picked through stones he found in the bottom of the creek bed. "I bet there's some valuable stones in here," Jeremy said. "Maybe I'll find gold!"

Dorie perched on the bridge and dangled her legs over the edge while she watched the boys and Corrie and Cassie Hammond, who picked wild flowers and pretty weeds along the creek. Every couple of minutes they ran up to Dorie and shoved the "pretty flowers" in her face for her to smell.

Chad looked up as a man approached the bridge from the direction of the parking lot. *Must be someone's dad.* He wore blue jeans and a tee shirt, hiking boots, and a Denver Broncos baseball cap. He stomped up to the bridge and stopped when he saw the children.

Dorie looked up and smiled. "Hi! Are you looking for someone in particular?"

The man stared at Dorie. She jumped up and leaned on the rail. Chad moved toward the bridge.

All of a sudden, a smile appeared as if by magic on his face. "Are you having fun?"

"We sure are," Jeremy shouted. "Playing in the creek is the best part of camp."

Chad nodded. "Yeah. And canteen."

Jeremy added some rocks to his pile on the edge of the creek. "But if any more food goes missing from the kitchen, we won't even get that."

"Food's missing from the kitchen?" The man leaned on the rail and smiled at Jeremy. "That seems unusual."

"Yep, it's a mystery," Chad said.

Chad looked at Dorie, and she barely shook her head at him. Dorie stood up as tall as she could and waved up toward the lodge. "Pastor Byrd, the director, is in there. I'm sure he would be able to answer any question or find anyone you need."

"Oh, that's all right." The man looked over toward the pond, where some of the campers were fishing. "I'm headed to my campsite at the campground down the road." He pointed on past the camp. "I thought I'd stop and see what was going on here."

"This is a church camp this week and next," Dorie said.

The man glanced up at the lodge. "So, you have missing food, huh?" He studied Dorie and Chad.

The kids just looked at him.

He shook his head. "Well, have a good afternoon." And with that, he marched back toward the road.

Chad watched him walk over to the parking lot, then shrugged his shoulders and went back to stomping in the creek. *Weird.*

Molly rubbed the pattern into her piece of shiny copper. The smell of paint and other craft supplies tickled her nose. She listened as chatter filled the upstairs craft room but didn't join in. Suddenly, footsteps pounded up the stairs. Molly looked up just as Chad whipped around the corner.

"Mrs. Hammond, we can't find Corrie. She's lost or something. Dorie sent me to get you." He said it all in a rush, his breath coming in gasps.

"You know Corrie, Chad. She probably hid in the bushes along the creek," Mrs. Hammond said.

"I'll watch the campers here," Aunt Susie said. "You go ahead."

"I think I know where she might be, Mrs. Hammond," Molly said. "I bet she went up the hill into the woods. She wanted to go get flowers this afternoon, but Dorie told her she would have to wait until tomorrow morning because they were going to play in the creek this afternoon."

"Into the woods by herself?" Mrs. Hammond's voice rose higher as she asked the question.

"Molly, Jeremy and me can show you where the flowers are," Chad said. "We went there lots last year."

"Let's go." Mrs. Hammond wiped her hands on a paper towel. "How did she get away without anyone noticing?"

"She said she had to go to the bathroom, and after a while, Dorie got worried," Chad said. "She sent Jeremy and me to look, but we couldn't find her."

When they got downstairs and outside, Dorie was running down the hill from the girls' cabins. "I checked all the girls' cabins, and Alex checked the boys' cabins. I'm sorry, Mrs.

Hammond; she wasn't gone more than ten minutes before I started to look."

"It's all right, Dorie. She's a stubborn, imaginative child, and she's a pro at disappearing. Molly thinks she may have gone for flowers." Mrs. Hammond grabbed Cassie and held her tight. "Do you know where Corrie was going, Cassie?"

"I don't know, Mommy. She said she hadda go to the bafroom."

"Okay," her mother said. "You stay here with Miss Dorie, and we'll go up the hill and look where the flowers are."

Pastor Byrd hurried down the lodge steps. "I'll go with you. We've checked the kitchen and all the playing fields. Let's go."

Pastor Byrd led the way up the hill with Chad and Jeremy on either side of him. Mrs. Hammond and Molly followed. They were barely out of sight of the buildings when they spotted the little girl. She stood with her back to them and waved into the woods. "Thank you, Cookie Monster," she called. "Thank you for bwinging me home." Then she turned and skipped toward the group. She stopped when she saw them.

"Hi, Mommy, I bwingded you some flowers. Here, smell them." She pushed the flowers into her mother's face. "I got kinda losted, but the Cookie Monster showed me the way." She pointed into the woods where she had come from.

"The Cookie Monster?" Corrie's mother hugged the girl tight and looked where the little girl had pointed. "Who is the Cookie Monster?"

"The man that bwought me back. He said his name was the Cookie Monster, and he said little girls shouldn't be in the woods by themselves; and he said if I would come to his kitchen tomowwo, he'd make me some cookies, but he couldn't wemember where his kitchen was."

"Uh-huh!" her mother said. "Is this like your friend Sophie?"

Jeremy giggled. "She's always making up friends who aren't real."

"No, Mommy. That's silly. No one but me can see Sophie; she's invisible. Invisible means you can't see them. That's Sophie. But the Cookie Monster, he's weal! He weared those pants like Daddy wears when he goes to the exercise place. He's tall, and he's old. But he was nice. He showed me the way home."

Pastor Byrd touched Corrie on the arm. "Honey, I don't know who brought you back, but we are glad. Did you get hurt?"

"No, I didn't get hurt. I didn't fall or nothing. I just went and picked my flowers, but then I couldn't wemember how to come back. I was sitting on a wock crying when the Cookie Monster said he would show me the way, and he did." She hid her face in her mother's shoulder. "I don't think I'll go in the woods alone again. I saw a weally big kitty, and he gwowled at me; but the Cookie Monster shouted at him, and he went away."

Molly's stomach lurched. *A really big cat? Could she have seen a mountain lion? Yikes!* She looked at Mrs. Hammond. Her face had gone as white as a sheet.

Pastor Byrd put his hand on Corrie's head. "Well, if you ever see this Cookie Monster again, Corrie, tell me. I'd love to thank him. Let's go. I think we better get back to the camp and let everyone know we found you."

"Thank you, God," Mrs. Hammond said. "And thank you, Mr. Cookie Monster."

CHAPTER 5

That evening at the campfire, the cousins all sat close to the fire on seats made from logs. Up on the top row of the bleachers, Max noticed Jess all alone. *I guess I should holler for him to come sit with us.* Just then, Slim climbed up and sat beside Jess. Max sighed. *I sure wish Jess was easier to like.*

Once the stragglers had arrived, Pastor Sting got up and led in some choruses. It was fun to hear their voices echo across the valley. The fire almost burned Max's face, but his back was chilly. The campers farther away from the fire huddled under blankets and jackets. "I wish we had some marshmallows," Max said to Carly.

Her eyes lit up. "That would be awesome."

After the choruses, Pastor Byrd stood up.

"God has taken care of us, and we survived the first full day of camp without any major injuries. He even protected little Corrie when she went into the woods. I would suggest— strongly—that you *not* wander into the woods by yourself. These are woods. Which means wild animals." He stopped until everyone looked at him, then smiled. "I also know you are excited about the idea of hidden treasure from the stagecoach robbery, so I've asked Alex to come share more about it, as well as our former cook's part in the exciting tale."

"All right!" Max could feel the excitement buzz around the circle of campers. Alex, a former camper, now came every summer to be a counselor. *I hope I can be as tall and strong as he is when I grow up.*

Several of the girls in the group giggled.

"That must be Alex's fan club," Brandon said. Max rolled his eyes.

Alex jumped up and rubbed his hands together. "Are any of you ready for a great campfire story?"

Cheers echoed throughout the valley.

"I guess so," Alex said. "Most of you know I'm in college, but do you know what my major is?" He looked around the group. No one said a word.

"Well, it's history. I can't get enough of history. I first learned about this stagecoach robbery when I was in the fifth grade. I live in Newcastle, and when we studied Wyoming history, we learned about the exciting things that happened back in the day. Lame Johnny's Gang and the Canyon Springs Stage Robbery of 1878 was—by far—my favorite."

Max leaned forward, his eyes never leaving Alex. The only sound was the crackle of the fire.

"Back then, Homestake Mine was *the* big business around here. They mined a lot of gold, and they needed to move it; but there were always those who wanted some gold for themselves. So, the company bought this super-duper coach called the *Monitor*. It was special-made with a five-sixteenth-inch metal plate on it, so bullets couldn't get through easily. They also had extra guards." Alex looked around the campfire and dropped his voice.

"But the best defense was the safe itself. It was said to be robber-proof. No way could *anyone* break into it. Want to know why?"

"Yes!" Chad shouted.

Everyone cheered.

Alex grinned. "Well, here's the deal. According to the manufacturer's warranty, it wasn't possible to get the safe open in less than six days unless you knew the combination."

A wave of chatter went around the campfire. "Wow," Max said.

"What happened then?" Peter called out from across the campfire.

Yeah. What happened? wondered Max.

Alex frowned. "Well, a gang led by Lame Johnny—whose real name was Cornelius Donahue—decided they wanted the treasure. So, when the coach arrived that day at the stage stop around the corner from here, they were waiting. They had surprised the attendant and tied him up in the barn. When the stage stopped and he didn't come out, one of the men went to look for the attendant. That's when the shooting started."

The hairs on Max's arms stood up, and he shivered.

"When it was all over, the passenger was dead; three from the stagecoach were injured; and one of the gang was wounded. He later died. While a stagecoach guard ran for help, the gang dragged the coach into the woods and started working on the safe. How long do you think it took them to open it?"

"Maybe they had the combination," Jess called out. "Maybe it was an inside job."

"That's a reasonable guess, but it wasn't what happened," Alex said. "Even without the combination, it took them only about two hours to open it."

An audible gasp rose from the campers.

"When help arrived, the gang was long gone, and so was the treasure. Now, this is where it gets even more interesting," Alex said. "The gang split up because one of them was too injured to travel fast. Eventually, they all died or were caught and punished, some by vigilante justice. Do you know what vigilante justice is?" Alex asked.

"That means when people take the law into their own hands," a boy called from across the circle.

"Yep. That's right. When all was said and done, they found sixty percent of the gold and most of the jewels and money. But there's still forty percent of the gold unaccounted for! A lot of people believe it's buried somewhere around here, and that's how our former cook comes into the story."

What a story! Max waved the smoke from his face. *The wind's shifted again.*

Alex nodded to the cousins. "If you need to move, you can."

"We're okay," Brandon said. "It will shift the other way soon."

"Okay," Alex said. "Back to my story. When I was a little kid, I came up for camp because my parents were workers. Like Chad and the Hammond kids."

Max looked over at where Chad and Jeremy sat with Slim and Jess. Chad's eyes were pinned on Alex, and Max could see him bouncing in his seat.

"Sometimes," Alex said, "Cookie—he was the cook—would lead the hikes, and occasionally, he would let me go along. Every single time, he would tell this story about when he was young. When Cookie—Mr. Sherwood—was a kid, he and his friend were exploring a cave up above the camp when they found some jewelry. They took it home and showed their parents, who took it to the authorities. Eventually, it was identified as some of the missing loot."

"No way!"

"That's awesome!"

"Wow!"

A general hubbub arose around the campfire until Alex lifted his hand.

"Of course, their secret cave was no longer secret, and a lot of people hiked up to search for the gold. The authorities even had to place a guard at the cave for a while, but nothing else was ever found! So, that's the true history of the stagecoach robbery, which happened right near here." Alex looked around. "Does anyone have any questions?"

"How much was the loot worth?" Dorie called out.

Alex nodded. "That's a great question. In 1877, it was worth over twenty-seven thousand, but now, it would be worth more like $1,750,000.00."

Once again, the campers erupted. Alex grinned at Pastor Byrd. "Now that I've got them wound up, it's your turn."

Pastor Byrd stood up. "Well, I can't follow that story with anything as exciting." Everyone laughed. "It makes me want to put my hiking boots on and go find some gold!"

A cheer arose, and the kids jumped to their feet.

Pastor Byrd shook his head and then motioned for them to sit down. When they had quieted, he said, "Don't even think about trying to find it while you are here. You can talk your parents into bringing you back to look if you want, but not this week. You might think it is funny to sneak out, but you won't think it's funny if I get ahold of you." He stopped and stared around at the campers, his face straight, no hint of laughter.

Max shifted in his seat.

Pastor Byrd smiled. "Now, I hope you'll sleep well tonight, since you're tired. Remember, there's to be no talking after lights out. I will not walk around tonight, but I'm sure I'll hear if some of you aren't quiet. Also, do not go outside of your cabins at night without a counselor. As you all know by now, we had a report of a large cat close to camp today. And I don't mean a kitty cat."

The campers laughed.

"We don't want any run-ins with wild animals. Anyone else have any announcements?" He looked around at the counselors. "Okay. That's it, then. Let's get some rest, so we can have a good Wednesday. Good night."

A few minutes later, Carly stood in the middle of their cabin. It was a chaotic scene. Girls climbed all over beds, some pulling clothes out of suitcases, others looking for items lost in the mayhem. Cindy shrieked when she tripped over a suitcase and fell onto her bunk.

"I have a plan," Aunt Susie said. "Everyone, get on your bed."

"But I'm not ready," Molly said.

"I know," Aunt Susie said. "You'll have time. Just get on your bunk now."

Once all the girls had settled on their beds, she explained. "When I say go, you will gather all of your stuff from around the cabin and put it on your bunk. I want your suitcases, your bags, shoes, teddy bears—*everything*—with you on your bunk by the time I count from ten down to one. Then, I'll tell you the next step. Ready?"

"Yes," chorused the girls.

"GO!" shouted Aunt Susie from her perch on the bed. "Whoa, girl, be careful," she said, as Carly dropped a shoe from her top bunk on Molly's head.

Within a couple of minutes, they were all back on their bunks, breathless and giggling.

"Now," Aunt Susie said, "I want you to put all of your clothes neatly in your bags—including your shoes, unless they're wet, in which case hand them to me, and I'll put them out on the porch under the eaves. Otherwise, everything in your suitcase will get damp and stink."

Carly wrinkled up her nose. "Here, Aunt Susie. I think mine better go on the porch."

Aunt Susie took the shoes. "The only things left out should be your pajamas and what you want to wear in the morning.

Hand me your Bibles and folders, and I'll put them on the table over here. Then we will put the bags in place on the floor, and clean-up will be simple in the morning."

"That's a good idea, Miss Susie," Leah said. She giggled. "I might need help, though. Someone may have to sit on my suitcase to close it."

When they had finished, Carly's mom stood by the door. "Does anyone need to go to the bathroom to brush your teeth or anything?"

"No," the girls chorused again.

"We will lock the door then," she said. "And remember what Pastor Byrd said—no one is to leave this cabin without a counselor."

Carly looked at her mother. *She's worried about something.*

After cabin devotions, the lights went out, and the girls settled down to sleep. Carly didn't hear anything from next door tonight. She watched out the window, her eyes getting heavy. *Either they're too tired, or they're scared they will be told to be quiet again.*

It seemed like she had just fallen asleep when the bell woke her up. *It can't be morning yet. That's the shortest night ever.* She opened her eyes and sat up. It was pitch dark. "It's not morning. Who rang the bell?"

"What time is it?" Leah mumbled.

"Midnight," Aunt Susie said. "Don't worry about it; we'll find out what happened in the morning. It didn't last long enough to be the emergency bell, so it must be a prank."

Carly shivered, pulled her sleeping bag up over her, and lay down, but she couldn't turn off her mind. *Too many weird things have happened. First, someone wandering around last night, food stolen from the kitchen, Corrie's Cookie Monster, and now this. Someone's up to no good.*

When the bell rang, Max had just laid down. A few seconds before, he was awakened from a sound sleep when the door opened. Jess stumbled into the cabin, his eyes half-closed. The noise didn't even stop Uncle Jeff's and Slim's snoring.

"Where did you go, Jess? Why didn't you get Slim to go with you?" Max whispered.

"I went to the bathroom; I forgot." Jess yawned. He had just gotten into bed when the bell rang.

Both boys sat straight up, and Slim wasn't far behind them. "What time is it?" Slim rubbed his face.

Max looked at his army watch. "Midnight."

"What's that about?" Slim asked.

"Another prank, I suppose," Uncle Jeff said. "If it were an emergency, it would still be ringing. All of our boys are here, aren't they?" He shone his flashlight around the room.

Max tensed and looked at Jess. *We are now.* Jess looked back, his eyes huge.

"Well, the bell will ring again soon enough; let's get some sleep," said Slim. The boys rolled over and tried to sleep, but it was a while before Max dozed off.

Did Jess really only go to the bathroom? Max couldn't get the brick out of the pit of his stomach. *I want to be a friend to*

Jess. After all, I learned a lot since last summer about not judging people. But what if Jess is up to something? He rolled over again. *God, please help me be a friend to Jess, and please don't let him be involved in something bad.*

CHAPTER 6

The next morning, Chad stood washing his hands at the bathroom sink outside the kitchen when he heard Pastor Byrd talking to Mr. Paul out in the hall.

"What was that bell all about last night?" asked Mr. Paul.

"Boy, wouldn't I like to know. By the time I got out of bed and looked out the window, no one was there. Only the swinging rope."

"I'm sure the caretaker will have something to say about it today." Mr. Paul laughed. "You know how he is about ringing it after nine p.m."

"I know," Pastor Byrd said. "That's the reason we don't ring it for lights out anymore. But that wasn't a mistake. Someone deliberately went out there and rang the bell at midnight. Someone is up to no good."

"Oh, tell me about it," Mr. Paul said. "Have you talked to Gilly today?"

"No, why?"

"You thought she was riled yesterday? Another loaf of bread is gone and a half gallon of milk. And whoever it is doesn't clean up at all."

"Oh no! I'll have to talk to the campers, I guess. Sounds like we have a thief and a prankster!"

"Well, if you want to know who I think it is, I'd suggest you start with Jess. He's been nothing but trouble."

"He's certainly a challenge," Pastor Byrd said.

Chad turned off the water as the men's voices faded.

They must have gone into the kitchen to talk to Miss Gilly. Boy, I have to tell Max and Carly about this. They didn't believe me before, but they will now.

Chad didn't even wait to dry his hands but dashed through the dining area and outside where the campers were lining up. He spotted his brother about four boys back from the front. Max slouched, hands in his pockets, hair standing up in all directions.

Chad rushed down the steps. As the words, "Max, I have to talk to you," left his mouth, he noticed who stood beside his brother. It was Jess. Chad stopped in his tracks, and his eyes widened.

"What's up, Squirt?" Max asked.

"Uh, can I talk to you?"

Max groaned. "Okay. But make it quick. The bell will ring any minute."

Chad pulled Max around to the side of the building and told him everything he had heard. "So, I wasn't crazy yesterday. Something *is* going on, and they think it's Jess."

"Well, I know for a fact Jess didn't ring the bell," Max said. "I'll tell Brandon and Carly. Listen and see what else you can find out." He gave Chad a fist bump. "You are pretty good at becoming invisible around adults. That's kind of handy. I'll have to call you Super Spy."

Chad stood up straighter, his shoulders back, and gave Max a salute. "I'll let you know if I hear anything else, Captain." Then he grinned. "Boy, will Germy be mad when he wakes up and finds out what he missed. I'm going inside to see if he's awake yet—and maybe jump up and down on his bed to help him wake up!"

When Max returned to the line, Pastor Byrd stepped off the porch. He didn't have the usual bounce in his steps or smile on his face. He pointed to the first boy in line. "Bill, please ring the bell."

As the bell rang, a few girls dashed down the hill, but Pastor Byrd simply watched and waited. Finally, he cleared his throat.

"I hate when we have to deal with problems at camp," he said. "Camp is a time when we get away, have fun, and learn more about Jesus." He looked at the campers, his face sad. "But today, we have a couple of situations which we must address."

He lifted a finger and said, First, someone rang the bell at midnight." He paused and looked around again. The campers were silent, their eyes fixed on him. "I know for a fact no leader rang the bell at midnight. For one thing, we are all so delighted to be asleep at midnight, we don't want to get up to ring a bell." The crowd twittered with giggles. "So, that means someone else did. I don't know who it was, but it better not happen again!"

"I bet it was Jess," muttered Peter.

Pastor Byrd stared at Peter until the boy dropped his eyes.

"The second—and more serious issue—is that someone has been sneaking into the kitchen at night and taking food and candy."

Brandon nudged Max's arm, and a quiet murmur rose around them as the campers talked among themselves. Pastor Byrd raised his hand.

"I have checked with the staff and the caretaker, and it wasn't any of them." He looked slowly around the group. "If this doesn't stop, we will not have canteen the rest of the week."

No one said a word. The only sound was banging pots from inside and the chirp of birds perched around the creek.

No canteen! Max looked across to Carly and Molly, who stared right back at him. Max knew exactly what they were thinking. *Yep, you guys are right. We have to figure out who is doing this.*

After Pastor Byrd dismissed them to go in to breakfast, Max pulled Jess aside. "Why did you leave the cabin by yourself last night?"

Jess glared at Max. "I told you last night. I went to the bathroom, that's what! Are you accusing me of something?"

"No." Max glared right back. "But it looks bad when you don't follow the rules and then something happens."

"Is there a problem?" Slim asked. Both boys jumped. They hadn't heard him coming.

Max looked at Slim, then at Jess. Jess kicked the ground with his foot, then looked at Slim. "I woke up last night and went to the bathroom. I forgot to have you go with me until I was halfway there. I didn't mean to break the rules." The words shot out of him, like a pop can that's been shaken. "I didn't ring the bell, honest. Max saw me come in before it rang . . . " Jess looked at Max.

"That's right," said Max. "He came in and barely got in bed before the bell rang."

"Were you in the kitchen?" Slim asked. "I know you will be asked when they find out you were out of the cabin."

"No, I wasn't." Jess shook his head. "Just the bathroom."

"He did look like he was half-asleep," Max said.

Slim looked from one boy to the other. "I believe you, Jess. But a lot of people suspect you, so you need to work extra hard not to give them any reason to believe you're involved."

"How can I do that? I get blamed for everything."

"Not if you follow the rules and hang around with kids who can vouch for you. Have you ever heard of an alibi?" Slim put his hand on Jess's shoulder. "You stay with Max and Brandon, or with me; don't leave the cabin without one of us; and they won't be able to blame you if something else happens, okay?"

"All right," Jess said. "Thanks, Slim, and you, too, Max."

"I know exactly how you feel," Slim said. "During our cabin devotions, I'll tell you my story. Then you'll see the value of hanging around good friends."

When Max and Jess got inside, the last campers were almost through the line. Max's stomach was growling, and he took some of everything that was offered. They hurried to get their food and found where the cousins were eating. At first,

Brandon, the girls, and Chad looked at Jess sideways. "He's with us from now on," Max said. "He needs to make sure he always has an alibi. He's getting blamed for stuff he hasn't done."

"Good idea," Carly said. "What can we do about the missing food?" She looked around the table. "We've got to do something. No canteen, no candy."

Brandon laughed. "That's a real problem for Carly," he said to Jess. "Carly loves her chocolate."

"So do I. Does anyone have an idea?" Max asked.

"There's something I didn't tell Slim. I didn't think about it until now," Jess said.

All eyes were on him. "When I went to the bathroom last night—"

"He was back *before* the bell rang," Max interrupted.

"Yeah," Jess said. "Anyway, someone else was already in the bathroom; and when I came out of the stall, he was gone, but so was my flashlight. I set it on the bench along the wall when I went in. There was some candy there when I walked in; but when I came out, the candy and my light were gone. I was too tired to mess with it, so I went back to my cabin."

"Do you think it was the person who rang the bell?" Molly asked.

Jess shrugged. "Maybe. Do you think it could be some of the missing candy?"

The group ate in silence for a little bit. "I guess we'll have to keep our eyes and ears open today." Max took a swallow of milk and attacked his French toast. "If we could watch tonight, it would be good, but we can't leave our cabins."

"We could stay up and watch out the windows," Molly said. "Then if anyone comes around the cabins, we may get a lead. But we're so far from the lodge, I'm not sure what we will see."

"We can see the kitchen door from our cabin," Brandon said.

"I guess that will have to do for now," Max said.

"Well, I'm buying two candy bars and no pop today," Carly said. She stuck out her jaw. "Just in case, I'll have some candy for tomorrow."

"Only if it isn't eaten today," Brandon said.

"Very funny." Carly smiled.

Jess perched next to Max on the porch rail of their cabin. They had finished cleaning in record time because Slim had promised to tell them about his past. The rumor had gone around that he was a train jumper for years. Jess shook his head. *That's hard to believe.* A thrill of excitement shot through him. *This might be the first time I actually like devotions.*

"Good job, guys," Slim said. "You were not only fast, but I think you might even deserve first place in cabin clean-up. If we leave the windows open today, it may not stink of dirty socks when we get back."

The boys laughed.

Slim sobered. "So, I promised to tell you my story today. I don't talk about it much, mostly because it's not something I'm proud of. It's not a cool saga about a kid on a grand adventure 'cause that's not how it was. I know there are lots of rumors going around. That I was a train jumper. That I ran away from home. That I lived like that for many years."

Jess glanced around. Every eye was on Slim.

Slim looked at each of them, one by one, ending with Jess. "That's all true."

Kevin gasped, then slapped a hand over his mouth.

Slim nodded. "Yes, it's pretty shocking, isn't it?" He laughed. "But what I want to talk about today is the before and after. 'Cause I sure didn't get up one day and decide my life goal was to be a train jumper for the next seventeen years."

Jess shifted on the rail. *Seventeen years! I haven't even been alive that long.*

"I had a great childhood," Slim said. "I had a loving family— my parents and my sister Michelle. We called her Mickey, and sometimes Mitsie." Slim grinned. "I liked to call her Minnie Mouse 'cause she's short, but she hated that." The boys laughed.

"My family are Christians; my dad's a deacon, and my mother is a Sunday school teacher. If the church doors were open, we were there, much like many of you. I didn't mind. It was all I knew. When I was nine years old, my first year at camp, I asked God to save me. And He did."

So what happened? I thought kids from "good homes" had it made. Jess looked at Max. He bit his lip like he knew what was coming.

"Life went along pretty well until I was seventeen. I'd met some new friends at school who weren't the best kids. My dad and I had started to butt heads some—partly because of my new friends, and partly because at seventeen, I had begun to get the idea that I knew more than my parents." Slim looked around. "Let me give you a life tool. When you're seventeen or eighteen, no matter what you think, you are not smarter than your parents."

A pained look flashed across his face. "I worked at the local hardware store. My dad was good friends with the owner, and he helped me get the job when I was fifteen. One day, when the owner counted the till, a hundred dollars was missing!"

Jess whistled. Slim said, "You're right, Jess. That's a lot of money. Since I was the one working the till, my boss assumed I was guilty. I denied it, of course, because I hadn't done it." His voice shook, and he stopped for a minute.

"See, it's still painful. I still get mad and have to ask the Lord to help me. I spent seventeen years mad about this, and that pattern doesn't just go away." He took a deep breath and continued. "What made me the maddest and hurt the worst was that my dad didn't believe me."

Slim stopped again for a minute and looked out over the boys' heads. Jess could see he was trying not to cry. When he spoke again, his voice was rough.

"So, I left. I decided if that's how Christians act, I didn't want to be one. I was never going home. If my dad didn't know me any better than that, then I didn't want him for a dad."

A huge lump almost choked Jess. He looked sideways at Max and noticed his eyes were wet.

"So, now you know how the story started. The middle was filled with temporary jobs, sleeping outside, in trains, in homeless shelters, or in the occasional hotel if I had the money. That was my life for seventeen years. Every year or so, I'd send a postcard home so Mom would know I was alive. Once, when

I was settled somewhere for a few months, she sent me a letter. She said they'd discovered who had taken the money, and my dad was sorry he didn't believe me. But I was still mad. I thought he should have believed me all along, and I couldn't let it go. I told myself I didn't care about my dad. I told myself I was living the life! But last spring, I got fed up with all of it. Seventeen years like that is hard. Hard," he said, his voice angry.

"One day, I was on a train, and we pulled into North Platte, Nebraska. All of a sudden, I had this urge to jump off, so I did. I walked a couple of blocks and came to a church. It was Pastor Jeff's." Slim nodded toward him. "He happened to be at the church, and I told him I wanted to find a job. He didn't make me feel lesser than him or like a bum, which was unusual. I often was treated bad 'cause my clothes were dirty and I looked scruffy. It was hard to find a place to shower, and no matter how hard I tried to keep clean, sometimes I smelled bad. You've seen homeless people before."

Jess nodded.

"He let me sleep in the church basement and called a rancher he knew, and I worked for him for a while. Then I went to the Johnson ranch, where I met Max and Brandon." He smiled. "It took me a while to let go of my wall of anger, but God and the cousins chipped away at it. Eventually, I called my parents, and they came to get me. There was a lot of forgiving to do, but God helped us. And now, here I am."

Slim looked around at the boys. "I want you to know, whether you are a church kid who may be a little bit tired of the Christian life, or maybe a kid who feels like an outsider—

maybe your family isn't the perfect family—I understand. God is the God of all of us. He knows you. He knows me. Before we end, I want to read from Psalm 139:1-12. This passage is one I memorized when I was a kid. Probably at camp or Vacation Bible School—I don't remember. Often, when I was traveling, God reminded me of these verses.

"O lord, thou hast searched me, and known me.

"Thou knowest my downsitting and mine uprising, thou understandest my thought afar off.

"Thou compassest my path and my lying down, and art acquainted with all my ways.

"For there is not a word in my tongue, but, lo, O Lord, thou knowest it altogether.

"Thou hast beset me behind and before, and laid thine hand upon me.

"Such knowledge is too wonderful for me; it is high, I cannot attain unto it.

"Whither shall I go from thy spirit? or whither shall I flee from thy presence?

"If I ascend up into heaven, thou art there: if I make my bed in hell, behold, thou art there.

"If I take the wings of the morning, and dwell in the uttermost parts of the sea;

"Even there shall thy hand lead me, and thy right hand shall hold me.

"If I say, Surely the darkness shall cover me; even the night shall be light about me.

"Yea, the darkness hideth not from thee; but the night shineth as the day: the darkness and the light are both alike to thee."

Slim closed his Bible. "If you ever think God doesn't notice you or you can run from Him, think again." Slim took two fingers and pointed to his eyes, then to the boys' eyes. "He's watching you. He knows what you think, say, and do. He knows exactly where you are physically, emotionally, and spiritually. You cannot run from God."

Jess shuddered. *God knows what I'm thinking? Right now? Boy, am I in trouble.*

CHAPTER 7

That afternoon, after canteen, Carly asked permission to go back to the cabin, where she hid the candy under her pillow. *There, now I'll have some tomorrow if they cancel canteen.* Carly stood for a couple of seconds in the silent cabin. After the hubbub of camp, the stillness was kind of nice. *It's stuffy and hot in here. Sure hope my candy doesn't melt.*

She hurried out the door, slammed it behind her, and galloped down the hill. When she rushed through the lodge doors, Coach Joe was dividing campers into groups for free time activities.

"Carly, over here," Molly called. Carly hurried to where Molly, Max, Brandon, Jess, Margaret, and Kevin gathered around Alex.

"Hi, Carly," Alex said. "I haven't had the chance to talk to you yet. How's camp going for you?"

"Fun! I said sections A, B, and C today in Bible memory time. Tomorrow, I'll try all of them at once. I'm determined to win the memory award this year."

"Good for you," he said. He looked around the room, then at the group of campers around him. "I think this is everyone. Let's review the rules. Stay together as a group. Max, we don't have another counselor today, and it's a small group, so would you bring up the rear? The rest of you, keep each other in sight and don't fall behind Max."

"Do we get to go to the lookout cliff?" Jess asked. "I heard it's the best view of the camp from up there."

"Yep, that's where we're headed. It's a little tougher hike, but I think it's worth it. Everybody have your water bottle?" The campers lifted their bottles for him to see.

"Good." Alex raised his hand. "Let's hike!"

They moved across the camp as a group until they came to the tree line. Max swatted a fly away from his face. *At least, it's not as hot as yesterday.* Once in the woods, the temperature dropped, and they settled into a single file line. Max brought up the rear. The chatter among the campers slowed as the climb got steeper. After a few minutes, the group had spread out so there were several yards between the front group and Max and Molly in the back.

"We need to hurry up, Molly."

"I can't go any faster!" Molly's breath came in short gasps. "It's too hard. My legs aren't as long as yours."

"It might be because you're always reading and doing crafty stuff," Max said. "You need more exercise to get in shape."

Molly stuck her tongue out at Max, and they both laughed.

They came over a rise and found Alex and the others resting. Alex gave each of them a high-five when they caught up. "This is the hardest part. You can make it, but I thought you might need a break. Besides," he waved his arm out in front of him, "look at the view."

Max turned, and through a break in the trees, he could see the camp.

"Wow," Brandon said, "the people look like miniatures."

Alex grinned. "Yep. That was a steep, fast climb. That's why you were out of breath, Molly. Drink some of the water you brought. That will help, too."

After a few minutes, he clapped his hands. "Let's get going. Holler up ahead if you need another break."

With that, the group moved off again. Molly waited until everyone else went ahead of her, except Max. "At least this way, I won't be in everyone's way if I'm slow," she said.

"You're doing all right. It's not much farther, anyway," Max said.

But a few minutes later, Molly was really lagging. When Carly disappeared ahead of them, Max looked around uneasily. "We've got to catch up, Molly. Here, hold my hand; I'll help." He grabbed her hand and pulled her along a little as they hurried ahead.

Around the next curve, both Max and Molly stopped dead in their tracks. In the middle of the path stood an old man. He was disheveled and looked tired. His sweat pants and plaid flannel shirt were filthy. He wore tennis shoes and carried a paper bag. Startled by the two young people, he dropped his bag.

Max bent down and picked it up. "Here you go, sir."

The man accepted the bag from Max, then stood up straight. Suddenly, it seemed he towered over them, and Max and Molly took a step back. "You youngsters better catch up." He waved up the trail. "It's not good to get separated from the group."

Max stared at the man, dumbfounded. In place of a weak, old man stood a tall, confident leader. It was the same man, Max knew, but his actions and demeanor had brought about the change. Instead of a dazed expression, the man's eyes were clear and alert. Without another word, he turned down the trail and soon disappeared around the curve.

Molly took off running up the trail, all of her tiredness gone. "Who was that?"

Max jogged behind her. "I don't know, but he's right. We need to catch up."

A couple minutes later, the pair heard voices and finally found the rest of the campers at the top of the cliff, gazing over the camp.

"What's wrong with you two?" Brandon asked. "You look like you've seen a ghost."

"It wasn't a ghost," said Max. "It was an old man. At least, he looked old at first."

"Yeah." Molly leaned over, hands on her knees to catch her breath. "He told us to get back with our group. He acted like he had seen you guys. Didn't you see him?"

Alex cocked his head sideways and looked at Max. "No, we didn't. You sure you saw him?" He laughed. "Or is this some kind of a trick?"

Max raised his hand like he was ready to be sworn in to testify at court and said, "No sir! I swear. There was a man on the path. He started back down the hill. Maybe we'll see him again."

"Maybe it was Corrie's Cookie Monster," Molly said.

Max stared at his cousins. *Oh, boy. This gets crazier all the time.*

The trip back to camp was mostly downhill, so they stayed together, but they had to be careful of shifting gravel under their feet. Max kept his eyes peeled; and when they got to the place where he and Molly had encountered the old man, he grabbed Alex's arm. "This is it," Max said.

Alex pointed to the trail leading off to the left. "That's the way to the cave where Cookie and his friend found the jewels."

"That was a cool story last night at the campfire!" Jess said. "Miss Gilly told us about Cookie and his friend yesterday. I guess Cookie liked to tell that story a lot. He even kept a newspaper article framed on the kitchen wall."

Alex laughed. "Oh, yes, he did! That was Cookie's one claim to fame." He smiled. "That and all the lives he changed through his ministry as a great cook and friend here at camp."

Just then, a middle-aged man appeared from the path to the cave. When he spotted the group, his eyes darted both ways, and he stopped in his tracks.

"Hello," Alex called. "We're from Camp Mallo; we've been out for a hike!"

The man nodded.

"Are you here with the older guy we passed earlier?" Molly asked.

The man's eyes jerked to Molly, and he smiled. "Why, yes, young lady. We're hiking some of the old areas my dad hiked when he was a kid." He pointed over his shoulder. "He's a little bit behind, but he'll catch up in a minute."

"Are you searching for the treasure from the stagecoach robbery?" Jess asked. Something in Jess' tone made Max look at him. His face was expressionless and his eyes a bit narrowed.

The man let out a short, harsh laugh. "Oh, that. My dad likes to dream about it. Two of his friends found some stuff up here when they were young, and Dad always hoped he could find something, too."

"Did your dad help a little girl find her way back to camp yesterday?" Carly asked. "She said he called himself the Cookie Monster."

The man shrugged his shoulders. "Could've been. He used to call himself the Cookie Monster with us when we were kids. Our name is Munster, so it was an easy leap—Munster, Monster." He shifted from one foot to another. "Well, I better backtrack a bit and see what's taking Dad so long. We should head back over to our campsite. You all have a great hike." He turned on his heel and stomped off toward the cave.

"Well, that solves the question about who the Cookie Monster is," Alex said. He waved his arm over his head in a circle. "Let's move out. We'll be late if we don't, and they'll send out a search party for us."

Max's feet hurried down the trail, but his mind stayed behind. *What is it about those two men that makes me nervous? I can't put my finger on it, but something is off.*

Back at camp, the kids hurried to their cabins to get cleaned up for the evening.

"Come back as soon as you're ready," Max said. "We need to come up with a plan for tonight."

"All right," Carly said. She and Molly dashed up the hill. "I've got to get a shower. I hope they aren't full."

"Me, too," Molly said. "I got my clothes out earlier, so I'll grab my stuff and go save us a place in line. I'll be on whichever side of the shower building is less busy."

"Thanks," Carly said. "That'll help a lot because I didn't get anything ready before."

"Hey!" Molly stood over her bunk staring at the blank spot on her pillow. "Pastor Byrd took my monkey!"

Carly looked over at her sister's bunk, then back at her own pillow where her stuffed cat rested peacefully. "He didn't take Muffy." She giggled. "Don't worry! He'll give it back at cabin inspection report. Either that, or it's outside in the trees or on the roof."

Molly dashed outside to look. "Here it is," she shouted from the side of the cabin. "He stuck Katie May up in the tree."

"That's a good place for a monkey," Carly said. All of a sudden, Carly remembered her candy bar. *He better not have taken that.* She reached over and lifted her pillow.

The candy bar was there, but the wrapper was chewed through, and part of the candy was gone. "Yuck!" She screamed, dropped the candy bar, and jumped back away from the bed, as if she had been bitten. "We have mice!"

"Mice?" Molly squealed.

Leah and Margaret appeared behind Molly in the doorway. "I left a candy bar under my pillow, and look at it." Carly held it up for all of them to see.

Aunt Susie appeared behind the girls. "That's why they say don't leave food in the cabin. I suggest you take it down to the trash can and throw it away." She looked around at the other girls. "If anyone else has any food in here, let's get rid of it now."

"I'm going to the shower, Carly," Molly said.

"Okay. I'm right behind you." Carly held the candy bar between her thumb and first finger like it was poisonous and marched out the door after Molly.

Forty-five minutes later, Carly and Molly arrived, hair combed but wet, at the picnic table by the sand volleyball court, where they had agreed to meet the boys. Chad, Jeremy, Max, Brandon, and Jess sat on the table benches.

Chad snapped his fingers. "So, what's up? It's super nachos tonight. I'm starving! Let's go."

Carly poked Chad's belly. "It's pretty flat. I guess you might need some food."

"You bet I do." Chad put his arms up to show his muscles. "I'm a growing boy!"

"Sit down, Chad," Max said. "We have about ten minutes until the bell rings for cabin inspection reports, and you won't miss supper."

Chad dropped to the bench with a thud and a heavy sigh.

"Two things," Max said. "What did you think of the younger guy we met in the woods, and do any of you have any ideas of what we can do tonight? We can't leave our cabin, that's for sure!"

"What guy?" Chad asked. Max filled Chad and Jeremy in on what had happened on the hike.

"He made me nervous," Molly said. "One minute, he didn't seem friendly at all; and the next, he was all smiling and nice."

"He made you nervous because he was nervous and maybe lying," Jess said. "He talked too fast, and his eyes went all over the place. He couldn't stand still either. That's not normal if you are telling the truth."

Max stared at Jess. "Where did you learn that?"

Jess shrugged. "On television shows."

"Well, I guess there's not much we can do about that," Carly said. "But what about tonight?"

"Germy and me can try to hang around the kitchen a little after campfire. If Mom lets us stay up." Chad grinned. "Mom's been letting me go to the campfire. We'll hang around the men, and maybe we can find out something."

"Good," said Max. "I guess the best we can do is watch out our windows tonight. If we can stay awake for part of the night, we might see something. I think it's happening during the first few hours after we go to bed."

"I hope I don't forget to get someone to go with me again tonight," Jess said.

"Maybe you can tie a string to your toe and to Max's; and that way, if you get up, he'll know it," Molly suggested.

"That's crazy," Brandon said. "Nobody really does that!"

"It might be crazy," Jess said. "But if something happens again tonight, I want to be able to prove I didn't do it. At this point, I'll try anything."

"My mom has string up in the craft room," Jeremy said. "I could get you some."

"That would be great. Thanks, Jeremy!"

When the bell rang, Carly got up. "I guess that's about all we can do for now. That and pray the real thief and prankster will be caught."

"Good idea!" Max said. "Let's each pray before we go to sleep tonight that it will be solved soon."

"Yeah!" Carly said. "I don't want to miss canteen tomorrow. Especially since I had to throw away a perfectly good candy bar because a mouse decided to climb under my pillow and eat it."

"You threw it away?" Brandon grinned. "You could have eaten the part he didn't touch."

"I don't think so!" Carly shuddered. "Yuck!"

That evening, the evangelist spoke about Caleb, a man who chose to follow God no matter what others said or did. "When the other spies said it was impossible to conquer the Promised Land," the evangelist said, "Caleb and Joshua said, 'With God, we can do it!' What about you?" He looked around the room at the campers. "Are you worried about what other kids will say? Do you let what others think make you do something you know is wrong? Do you believe God is all-powerful and can help you do whatever He wants you to do?"

Max squirmed in his seat. *Can he read my mind? I know I don't like the other guys mad at me about Jess.*

At the end of his message, the speaker had everyone bow their heads while he finished his application. "Caleb could stand firm in what he believed because he trusted God. He knew God. He knew the power of God. The only way we can know God is if we have received the Lord's gift of salvation. Maybe you have never done that. Tonight would be the best time for that. Then you can have God's help when you are faced with questions and problems."

Max sat beside Jess, his head bowed. *Lord, I'm sorry I've been more worried about what the guys think than about Jess. I don't think Jess knows you.*

Jess shifted in his seat and swung his legs back and forth. When the evangelist asked everyone who wanted to receive Christ to stand and go to the back of the room, Max held his breath. Jess sat frozen, his hands gripping the chair seat so hard, Max could see his knuckles were turning white.

He leaned over and whispered, "Do you want me to go with you?"

Jess's head jerked sideways, and he looked at Max. Finally, after what seemed like a couple of minutes to Max (but was probably only a few seconds), Jess nodded.

The two boys got up and made a beeline for Slim, who stood at the back with the other counselors.

"I want to ask God to save me," Jess said. "Max came along for moral support."

Slim put an arm around each boy. "Let's go out to the picnic table, and we'll talk about this some more."

CHAPTER 8

A few minutes later, the campers sat on the bleachers and logs around the campfire. After the singspiration and missionary time, Pastor Byrd asked if anyone had a testimony. "Usually, we wait until Friday night for those, but I wondered if anyone wants to share tonight."

No one said anything for several seconds, until Jess stood to his feet. He looked down at the ground, then up at Pastor Byrd. "I'm thankful for a friend like Max, who stood up for me when a lot of others didn't. He even went with me tonight to talk to Slim, and I asked Jesus to forgive my sins. I don't think I would have done that if he wasn't my friend. That's all." He plopped back down by Max.

Pastor Byrd smiled at Jess. "That's wonderful, Jess! Thank you for sharing with us. You'll find it is the best decision you'll ever make!" He paused a moment. "We don't usually address the gossip that goes on at camp, but I think this needs to be said. Several people have suggested that Jess is responsible for the pranks and missing food."

There was silence, and you could have heard a pin drop on the soft dirt. Jess bit his lip. What would Pastor Byrd say?

"Jess was in his cabin when the bell rang. I am convinced he isn't responsible for these incidents. I don't know who is—I don't even know if it's a camper or not—but it's not Jess." After another short pause, Pastor Byrd ended the campfire with this reminder. "Remember, tomorrow's water day. Dress appropriately and get some good sleep. You'll need it."

"Jess, wait a minute." Jess, Max, and Brandon, who were headed back to their cabin, turned to find Chad and Jeremy pushing through the crowd of campers toward them.

Jeremy held out his hand. "Here's some string. My mom wanted to know why I needed it, and I told her it was for a safety issue." He laughed. "She rolled her eyes and told me to be careful."

"A safety issue." Max gave Jeremy a high-five. "That's a good one. Thanks. We'll let you know in the morning how it worked." He dropped his voice and looked around. "Keep your ears open, and we'll compare notes in the morning."

"I haven't been taking any notes," Jeremy said, a worried look on his face.

Jess laughed. "No sweat. He means we'll see what's new, you know?"

An hour later, the only sound in the camp was the burbling creek, a few birds, and the cicadas, who were announcing that summer would be over in a few weeks. Most of the campers had given in to exhaustion and were already asleep. Carly and Molly sat up on their bunks and stared out the windows. Carly could tell from their breathing that even Aunt Susie and her mother were asleep. *This is so boring, and I'm wiped out. There's nothing happening out there. We're too far from the lodge to see anything, anyway.*

A few minutes later, Carly was about ready to lose her battle against sleep when Molly whispered, "Someone's out there."

"Who?"

"I don't know; I can't see. Wait a minute. I think it's Pastor Byrd and Coach Joe. Yep, it's them. They're carrying a stick. Or maybe . . . no, I think it's a flashlight, but it's turned off."

"They must be guarding the camp," Carly said.

Scratch, scratch, scratch. Carly caught her breath.

"What's that?" Molly asked. The noise stopped as soon as she spoke. The girls waited and listened. *Scratch, scratch.* "There it is again."

Again, the girls sat in silence until the noise returned.

"What is it?" Molly asked again, this time her voice louder.

"What's wrong?" Their mother sat up. "What's going on?"

"There's something in the cabin," Carly said. "We hear it whenever we stop talking." They fell silent again, and sure enough, the persistent scratching returned, this time followed by a thump.

"I think it's coming from the trash can," Leah said.

By now, all the girls in the cabin were awake, as well as the two counselors. Aunt Susie got up, turned on the light, and went over to the trash can.

"Well, look what we have here." She put her hands on her hips. "We have a poor, little, trapped visitor."

Carly jumped off her bunk and gathered around the can with the rest of the girls. In the bottom of the metal container cowered a small mouse, doing his best to hide under the candy wrappers, which had attracted him.

A couple of the girls screamed and fled back to their bunks. Cindy covered her head with her blankets. "I hate mice," she said, her voice muffled.

"Oh, he's cute," Carly said. "I bet he was trying to climb the sides, and that's what we heard."

"Don't kill him," Molly said. "It's not his fault we're in his house this week. He could be a cousin of Ralph S. Mouse."

Aunt Susie laughed. "I doubt it, but I'll take him down the path and let him go." She slipped on flip-flops. "Carly and Margaret, do you want to go with me?"

"Sure," the girls said. They grabbed their flip-flops and followed Aunt Susie out onto the porch.

"Awk!" the girls screamed. Even Aunt Susie gave a little shriek. Standing at the bottom of their steps were two men, each holding a huge flashlight.

"Pastor Byrd, you scared us to death," Aunt Susie said. "What's wrong?"

"That's what we wondered," Pastor Byrd said. "We were making our rounds, and we saw your light come on. Then we heard screams." His eyes fell to the trash can. Aunt Susie held it out so he could see.

Carly giggled.

"This little guy is the reason for this whole ruckus," Aunt Susie said. "We're going to liberate him a little way down the path. We don't want to kill him, but we don't want him in our cabin again either."

The men's faces relaxed, and they laughed, too. "Okay. Well, hurry up; it's late."

"You can count on it!" Aunt Susie said. The two girls and their counselor held onto each other and hurried down the path, where they let the mouse run off into the grass.

Brandon and Max watched out the window that faced the bathroom while Jess monitored the kitchen door from his window across the room. Slim and Uncle Jeff snored softly. Several minutes had passed since Jess had seen Pastor Byrd and Coach Joe walk by the other side of the cabin.

"Hey, Max. Do you see that?" Brandon whispered. He pointed toward Cabin One up the hill. It was empty, since they had enough room in the other cabins. "There's a light up there."

Max leaned toward the window, staring into the darkness. "I don't see a light." He rubbed his eyes and looked again. "Wait. Yeah, I see it. Someone's there."

"Maybe some of the visitors that were here for the midweek service stayed, and they put them in there," Jess whispered. "Some of the people from my church were here. Pastor canceled the Wednesday service because he couldn't be there to preach since he's here at camp."

Slim rolled over in his bed, and Max froze. Once Slim started snoring again, he relaxed. Max looked at his watch, pressing the button that lit up the face. *Almost midnight.* Brandon reached across from his bed and grabbed Max's arm, looked at the watch, and settled back onto his bed.

"The light's gone," Max whispered. "Ouch." The string tied to Max's toe jerked. He looked across the room, and Jess motioned for him to lie down. As he flopped down on the bed, he heard quiet steps on their porch, followed by a soft knock on their door.

"Slim," Max said. "Someone's at the door."

"Huh? What?" Another soft knock. Slim jumped out of bed and hurried to the door. He opened it a crack and whispered, "I'll be out in a minute."

"What's up?" Brandon asked.

"We're taking turns patrolling tonight, Brandon. Go to sleep. I'll be back in a couple of hours."

Max lay in bed, his eyes wide open. *They must be worried the prowler isn't a camper 'cause if they thought it was, they wouldn't need to patrol. They would just put someone in the kitchen.* Max stared out the window at Cabin One. *I'll watch that door all night. If anyone comes out, I'll know it.*

At 5:30, the dim light filtered through the trees in the window, and Max woke up. He rubbed his eyes to clear the blurriness. As they focused, movement on the porch of Cabin One made him bolt upright. Only a flash, then it was gone as someone closed the door. There *was* someone there. *If I'd stayed awake . . .* A flash of orange in the shadows above the cabin caught Max's attention. Movement. He narrowed his eyes, trying to see better in the early dawn light. *Someone is watching the cabin. Maybe a counselor?* He squinted. The shadowy figure was gone. He groaned, rolled over, and covered his face. *I might as well sleep now.* He glanced over to Slim's bed and saw his head covered with a pillow. Max hadn't heard him come in. *I wonder if they saw anything.* He rolled over and went back to sleep.

At 7:20, Chad and Jeremy already hung over the porch railing, waiting for flag-raising. When the bell rang, the campers straggled into line. A few minutes later, it was a sleepy-looking group that gathered at the table with Mrs. Hammond and Mrs. Rawson. Chad and Jeremy were the only ones eating with their eyes open.

Chad poured syrup on his French toast. "Boy, is Miss Gilly mad this morning."

Max's head snapped up. "Why?"

Chad looked around, pleased with the attention his statement attracted.

"You tell them, Germy," he said. "I'm hungry." He smirked at Jeremy, stabbed a piece of French toast with his fork, and put it in his mouth. Then he put down his fork and licked his fingers.

Max rolled his eyes and looked at Jeremy. "Let's hear it."

"Well, I don't know. I don't tell things as good as Chadstick." He took a swallow of milk, then picked up his fork.

"Jeremy!" his mother said. "Spit it out."

Jeremy shrugged. "Well, we overheard Miss Gilly talking to Pastor Byrd and Pastor Hall. It was easy to hear 'cause she was so mad, she almost hollered."

"Yeah." Chad looked at his mom, then swallowed what he had in his mouth. "We were up by the piano when she started. Someone was in the kitchen again last night. No, I think it was this morning. Anyway, they left a mess and a burner on with a pan on it. Miss Gilly shouted that the place could have burned down again like it did when she was young and about how someone named Cookie would be utterly disgusted. Those were her words—'utterly disgusted'—with how this week is going. I don't know who this Cookie is, but she mentioned him several times, like he was the boss or something."

The group sat in shocked silence. Max stared at his brother. Miss *Gilly mad? Mad enough to shout? Unbelievable. She's such a happy person.*

"Cookie used to be the cook," Jess spoke up. "Miss Gilly mentioned it when we were in the kitchen. Don't you remember, Chad?"

"Oh, yeah," Chad said. "I forgot. Anyway, the men patrolled until about four, and Miss Gilly said she was in the kitchen at 5:30. Pastor Byrd said they checked the kitchen last thing. So, the thief came in sometime in there."

"Someone was up by Cabin One about 5:30," Max said. "I saw the door close, and I thought there was someone above the cabin in the trees." He yawned. "But when I looked again, they were gone. It was too dark to see well."

Carly put her face in her hands. "I guess we won't have canteen today."

"We'll have to see about that!" Max said. "Anyone else see anything last night?"

"A mouse." Molly giggled. "We had a mouse in our cabin. It woke everyone up, and some of the girls were screaming."

Carly lifted her head. "Then when Aunt Susie, Margaret, and I went outside to let it go, Pastor Byrd and Coach Joe scared us about half to death. There they were, standing in front of our cabin. They heard the screams and came to check on us."

Brandon grinned. "I wish I had been there to see it."

Carly made a face at him. "If I didn't know better, I'd think you put that mouse there, smarty pants."

They were interrupted by Pastor Byrd with morning announcements. "Good morning, campers."

"Good morning," chorused the campers and counselors.

"I am sorry to announce that someone has been in the kitchen again. This time, they left a pan on the stove and the burner on. If anyone knows anything, please let me know. Because of that, we will not have canteen this afternoon unless it's cleared up."

Carly groaned. "I'll have chocolate withdrawals."

"Bring your cat to the morning session for the stuffed animal contest," Molly suggested. "You know everyone who participates always gets a snack-size candy bar."

Carly perked up. "That's a good idea, Molly."

"I have an idea," Max said. "Meet me at the table for a minute after cabin devotions. I need to tell you something I saw."

CHAPTER 9

"I know someone went into Cabin One at 5:30, and someone was watching it. I think we should check it out," Max said on their way to cabin clean-up.

"But what if the person is supposed to be there?" Brandon asked.

"I looked around this morning. There weren't any visitors at breakfast," Max said. "If they spent the night, they would have been at breakfast."

"Unless they left early," Jess said. "That could be why they were up so early. Maybe they headed back to town to work."

"That's true," Max said. "But if so, the cabin should be empty now. I still think we should check it out. If it was visitors, we don't want to make a big deal out of nothing." He stopped where the path turned to go up to Cabin One. "You know how the schedule is. If we don't go now, we won't have another chance until right before supper."

Jess shook his head and held his hand up. "*I'm* not going in there. If someone saw me, they would think the worst. I'll go to the cabin, and you two run up there. I'll tell Slim you were delayed or something. Plus, if you need help, shout for us. Then I can get Slim and come see what's up."

"Smart! We'll be there in a minute," Max said.

Jess hurried to their cabin, and Max and Brandon slipped up to Cabin One. They had waited until the last minute when everyone else was busy cleaning; but even so, Max was nervous. As they approached the cabin, they walked slower and stopped talking. Max thought his heart would beat right out of his chest. They crept up onto the porch, gently opened the door, and peered into the dim room where the smell of old socks and dirty clothes smacked them in the face. Max wrinkled his nose. He scanned the room as they stepped through the doorway. "No one," Max said, both disappointment and relief in his voice.

Brandon walked around the room. "Someone was here, though." He picked up a flashlight. On the handle, in black ink, was written "Jess Carter."

"Well, it wasn't Jess this morning," Max said. "His toe was tied to mine with that string, *and* he was in his bed."

"I know," said Brandon. "But this explains where his flashlight went the other night."

Max glanced into the trash can. "Hey, look at this!" He held up the can, turning it so Brandon could see the inside from across the room. In the bottom were a bunch of candy wrappers. Empty candy wrappers.

Brandon and Max stared at each other. "Someone has been in here, that's for sure," Max said. "Now we have to figure out who! We better get back to our cabin now, though, or Slim will come after us."

Brandon, flashlight in hand, started for the door. "I'm taking this to Jess. He doesn't need someone else to find it here."

"Boy, you're right about that!" The boys peered around the door and waited until they couldn't see anyone on the path before they left the cabin. A few seconds later, they rushed into their cabin.

"Sorry we're late." Max hurried over to his bed, grabbed his pajamas, and stuffed them in his suitcase.

Brandon handed the flashlight to Jess, who was straightening Brandon's sleeping bag. "Thanks, Jess, you didn't have to do that. I owe you one now."

The boys avoided looking at Slim, but Max could feel his eyes on them. Jess shoved the flashlight under his pillow and grabbed the trash can. "I'll go empty the trash. Do you want me to see if I can find a broom?"

"Sure," Slim said. "We'll let Max sweep, and Brandon can mop, since they waited so long to show up." Max glanced at Slim. He looked Max right in the eye, a slight smile on his face, his right eyebrow lifted.

"Sounds fair to me," Max said.

"Slim wasn't fooled for a minute." Max frowned. "He knows we're 'up to something'—as Grandpa Johnson would say—but he doesn't know what." The group once again lounged around the picnic table.

"Where's Jeremy?" Carly asked Chad.

"His mom went to town for supplies, so she made him go with her. She said she wanted some company. He said he'll try to get her to talk about the counselor meeting to see if she knows something we don't know."

Dorie pushed her hair back from her face. "Well, that boy can sure talk your leg off. She might let some piece of information slip in self-defense." She leaned forward. "I saw something this morning. When I got up, I went out on the back porch about 5:30, and there were two people hiking up the hill above Cabin One."

"Together?" Max asked.

Dorie shook her head. "I don't think so. It looked to me like one of them was following the other. They were too far away to see well, but the one who followed looked familiar."

"What about those two men we ran into on our hike?" Max asked. "Maybe it was them."

"But the younger one said they are staying at the campground," Carly said.

Dorie shook her head. "I didn't get the idea the first one knew he was being followed." The kids sat in silence for a minute.

"Maybe it was a couple of the pastors going for a hike," Molly said.

"They should play the games with us," Jess said. "I bet then they would be too tired for morning hikes."

"Let's go," Brandon said. "If we're late again, Slim will hang us by our toes until we tell him what's up."

Max grabbed his stuffed snake to take into the lodge. "Did you all bring your stuffed animals?" They each held up their animal.

Even Jess had a stuffed spider. "I thought maybe I could scare some girls with it."

When they went up the steps onto the lodge porch, they walked past a line-up of counselors, waiting for Coach Joe to arrive with the water balloons. "We're filling a bunch so we can drench you kids," Alex called. "You better be prepared."

"Just you try," Jess said.

Chad stayed outside when the others went in for the missionary lesson. "Hey, Slim." Chad climbed up on the rail so he could see.

"Hi, Chad. How's it going? Where's your sidekick?"

"Who?"

"Your sidekick, Jeremy. It seems you guys are always together, except early in the morning. He doesn't seem to be as much of a morning person as you are."

"I like mornings," Chad said. "It's the best part of the day. Germy went to town with his mom. He's going to ask her questions about . . . " Chad stopped. *Uh-oh. I almost blew that.* "Can I help you with the balloons?"

Slim didn't say anything for several seconds, while Chad held his breath. Finally, Slim patted Chad on the back. "Sure. Your Aunt Susie is going to help me, too. Let's find us a water spout, and we'll be in the water balloon business. Then you can tell me what this water day is all about. I keep hearing water day, water day, water day."

"Okaly dokaly." Chad jumped off the rail. "They play all kinds of games with water. Tug of war over the creek; duck, duck, splash, where you dump a bucket of water on the person's head instead of tapping them; slip and slide—they put the team in a row and make them pass a bucket of water over their heads." Chad rambled on as he paced around the porch. "Then they play games in the field. Toss the balloon, stuff like that." He stopped in place. "But the best part is when they use this humongous slingshot to try and hit the archery shed with the water balloons." He bounced up and down. "The grand finale is a massive water balloon fight, and someone always seems to end up in the creek."

Slim scratched his head. "Wow! That's a lot of water activities. Do you ever get wet, or do you just have to watch?"

Before Chad could answer, Coach Joe arrived with his pickup, and the counselors flocked around it. Chad hopped up in the back and grabbed three five-gallon buckets and a bag of balloons. "Here." He handed them to Slim. "I'll show you how we do it. The best place to fill balloons is that faucet." He pointed to the wall by the kitchen.

"For sure, he's a pro, Slim." Coach adjusted his cap. "This boy has helped with balloons since he was about four. I do believe it's the highlight of his week." He put his hands on his hips. "What will you do for the next eight or nine years when you're a camper and can't help?"

Chad's mouth dropped open. "I don't know. I guess I'll have to miss it. Maybe they'll let me help during one of our free times."

Slim laughed. "I think you will have enough new fun that you won't miss it too much. And when you grow up, maybe you can be the coach, and then you can fill all the balloons you want."

At lunch, the dining hall was even noisier than usual. The chatter was all about the afternoon activities. Water day would be the last event of the afternoon, so the campers could go straight to the shower. "I heard they are going to do the airsoft, kickball, and geocaching activities during the first recreation hour today," Max said.

"It's our turn for geocaching," Carly said. "We've done the other two."

"I'm not even sure what geocaching is," Molly said.

Brandon rubbed his hands together. "It's really cool. It's like a treasure hunt, only you use a GPS."

"Well, I guess we'll find out this afternoon," Carly said. "First, we learn verses, though. I think I'll be able to say the first three sections together. Then, I'll say the other sections by themselves. Tomorrow, I hope I can say all of it at once."

"Wow," said Jess. "I can't get past the first section."

"You have to concentrate and shut out all the noise and activity around you," Max said. "I'm not as good as Carly, but that's what works for me."

"I'll try it," Jess said. "I want to learn as many as I can in the next two days."

After memory time, the kids huddled in a circle with their notebooks to compare how they had done. "I did it!" Carly lifted her arms in the air. "I said the whole book. Not at once," she added. "Maybe tomorrow."

"That's awesome," Molly said. "I said three sections verse by verse, but tomorrow, I'll try to say section one all at once."

"How did you do, Jess?" Max asked.

Jess held up his book, so they could see the front. Max whistled. "Three stars? You said three sections, each section all at once? Boy, you *can* memorize."

Jess grinned. "I did what you suggested. I sat by myself, tuned everyone out, and memorized. Then, when I knew it, I went and said the verses to Slim." Jess's eyes shone. "I didn't think I could, but I did!"

Max gave him a high-five. "You'll have to watch out next year, Carly," Max said. "I think you have some new competition."

Teams One and Five did go geocaching in the woods. Using a GPS, they found all of the hidden "treasures" except for the last one. When they came back to the lodge after the bell rang, they were hot, tired, and hungry. "Too bad we didn't find the fake pine cone," Carly said. "We would have if we'd had a few more minutes."

Max rubbed the sweat from his face with his t-shirt. "Of course, we didn't find it. How can you find anything with silly eyeball glasses with just a pinpoint opening to see through?"

Molly giggled. "I bet we looked hilarious, crawling around the ground with pinpoint vision."

"The rest were pretty easy," Carly agreed. "I'm sure they did that to make it harder. It sure was fun, though! I think that and the Capture the Flag game with the airsoft guns were my favorites so far." She held her hair up off her neck. "I sure wish we could have canteen. I'm starving and dying of thirst."

"May I have your attention!" Pastor Byrd stood by the serving tables. The campers eventually quieted. "We have an activity now which I think you'll like. Something we've never done before. I'll let Coach explain it to you."

Coach bounded to the front, a large shopping bag in his hand. "Are those what I think they are?" Carly whispered to Molly. "They look like packages of cookies." Her stomach grumbled.

Coach took one out of the bag and held it up. "We will now have the first ever Oreo cookie challenge. I want you to divide up into your teams and find a spot at a table."

A general stampede ensued, and the campers quickly sorted themselves into teams.

"Okay," Coach said. "Now, we will give each team a box of family-sized double-stuffed cookies. When I say go, you can open the package and divide the cookies up among your team."

"Wahoo!" Carly shouted. "Chocolate."

The lodge erupted with cheers and laughter. Pastor Byrd pointed to Carly. "And no, Carly. You can't eat all of them for your team."

Coach laughed. "That's right. You have to divide them as evenly as you can among your team members. There are," he stopped to look at the bag, "forty-eight cookies in each container."

Counselors carried pitchers out from the kitchen and placed them around the tables.

"We have water for you to drink, too," Coach said. "So, let's get started."

Within ten minutes, it was all over. Carly sighed. Her team hadn't won; but her stomach was full, and her chocolate craving was satisfied.

"I think they did this since we can't have canteen," Brandon said. "I don't think they believe one of the campers is taking the food."

Carly nodded. "I bet you're right. I hadn't thought of that." She giggled. "I was just so happy to see those cookies."

It's scorching this afternoon. There's not even a breeze out here. Max waited in line for his turn to use the water balloon slingshot. He watched as two campers held the sides of the slingshot, and Jess put the water balloon in, pulled back as far as he could, and aimed. The balloon flew through the air, across the field, and hit the archery shed.

"Way to go, Jess," Max shouted along with the other teammates. Suddenly, something warm ran down his upper lip. He wiped it off and glanced at his hand. It was blood. He pinched his nose and headed toward his mom, who sat in the shade of an RV.

"I hab a bloody dode," he said. Blood dripped from his hand. His mother pulled a paper towel from her bag and poured some cold water over it.

"Here, sit down," she said. "Use this to wipe your hands off; I'll hold your nose." She pinched on either side, halfway up the nose.

"It stops the bleeding faster if you push up here. The blood vessels travel through there."

Once he had his hands clean, she let him hold pressure and got a clean paper towel wet. "Now, put this between your eyes." She held a small ice bag on the back of his neck. He shivered, but it felt so good in the heat.

"Does Max get a lot of bloody noses?" Aunt Susie asked.

"No," his mom said. "But when you get so hot, and the air is so dry, it's not uncommon. The campers should be drinking more water."

"I think this is the first year since I can remember where Thursday has been hot," Aunt Susie said. "Usually, Water Day is the coolest day of camp. Cool and rainy—that's what often happens."

"Not today," Max's mom said. "Their faces are so red, even with their wet clothes."

"What's wrong?" Chad and Jeremy plopped down on the ground beside Max.

"Oh, he has a bloody nose," Mrs. Rawson said. "Hi, Jeremy, did you have a good time in town?"

He shrugged. "I guess so. It was fun until Mom read the front of the paper in the store and burst into tears. She's still up in the kitchen crying with Miss Gilly."

"What's wrong?" Max's mom asked.

Jeremy shrugged. "Something about some man who's missing. An old man. He has Ochenzimers, or something like that. He left the place he lived, and they can't find him."

Max let go of his nose and looked at Jeremy. "Was it someone your mom knows?"

Jeremy nodded. "She said he was the camp cook. His name is Carl, I think. Miss Gilly—she's more upset than Mom. She took off her apron and was ready to go to town and look for him."

"Oh, no," said Max's mom. "That's Cookie."

"Cookie?" Max asked. "That's the guy who was cook here."

His mom sat down by Max and pulled her legs up to her chest, her chin on her knees. "Cookie," she said, a little smile on her face. "That's what everyone called him. We all loved him. He treated each of us as if we were his favorite."

Aunt Susie chuckled. "But don't even think about taking more than two cookies when he was at the window."

Max's mom shook her head. "Oh no! Then he turned into another Cookie."

"What would he do?" Chad asked, his eyes wide.

"Two cookies. I said two cookies!" Aunt Susie bellowed the words, her voice deep. Max, Chad, and Jeremy all jumped.

"You all okay over there?" Slim called from Max's line.

Aunt Susie giggled. "We're fine! Never mind us!"

Chad bounced up. "That's the man Miss Gilly was talking about the other day. She said he talked her into helping in the kitchen, and that's why she's the cook now."

"It's no wonder she's sad," Max's mom said. "Cookie was like a father to Miss Gilly."

Chad nodded. "Yeah, she told us that."

"Did the newspaper give any details?" Max's mom asked. "Like how long he has been missing, if they have any clues to where he might go, anything like that?"

Jeremy shrugged. "I don't know. Mom just started bawling and said she had to get back and tell Miss Gilly. She bought the paper. They're all in the kitchen taking turns reading the article and crying. I had to get out of there. All that crying was depressin' me."

Max's mom looked at his nose. "Looks like it's stopped, doesn't it?"

Max removed the paper towel and waited a few seconds. "I think so."

"I'm going up to the kitchen to talk to Miss Gilly," she said. "If anyone needs me, that's where I'll be. It looks like they're about ready for the grand finale here, anyway, and I don't want to get wet."

Aunt Susie stood up, too. "I'll come with you." She looked at Max. "Tell Carly I've got her camera and her watch." She held them up. "I'll meet them back at the cabin in a few minutes. I'm not too excited about a water fight either."

"Ah, you're chicken." Max pulled a water balloon out from inside his shirt and pulled his arm back to throw it at her.

"Don't you dare," she shouted. "If you throw that, I'll . . . "

At that instant, a bucket of water flooded over Max's head. He cringed at the unexpected shower, then rolled sideways and leapt to his feet to face his attacker. It was Slim.

"Just protecting my lady," Slim said. "Looks like you can come back and join the team now." He grabbed Max's hand and pulled him to his feet. "Let's go, big guy!"

Max stood stock still, shocked at the sudden turn of events. His mother was bent over at the waist laughing. Chad and Jeremy hopped around whooping at the top of their lungs. Aunt Susie had turned beet red.

"Honey," his mother said, between giggles. "I think that should help you cool off." With that, she and Aunt Susie jogged toward the lodge. Max shook the water out of his hair as he followed Slim back over to his team. He could hear his mom and Aunt Susie laughing halfway up to the lodge.

CHAPTER 10

"I told you to take a shower," Peter said. He grinned at Max. It seemed the entire camp had heard about the dunking Max had taken. Max laughed and shook his head.

"He got me good, that's for sure. I didn't see him coming at all."

The campers waited in front of the lodge for supper, the excitement level still high from the Water Day activities.

"You should see our front porch," Carly said. "There are so many wet clothes on the rail, they are piled two-deep. I don't know how they will ever get dry before we leave Saturday."

"My mom sent a plastic bag," Max said.

"Oh, mine did, too," Carly said. "The mess we had last year won't soon be forgotten at our house."

"Last year!" Max hooted. "You mean, when you fell in the lake trying to outrun the little kids chasing you with their balloons?"

Carly's face turned a distinct color of red, and she put her hands on her hips. "I tripped," she said. She giggled. "But, boy, was I drenched. And the slimy mud and weeds in my clothes— that's what made Mom so upset." Carly raised her hand and announced to the gathered campers, "So, I'm here to tell you, if you ever fall in the lake, rinse your clothes out before you go home. Better clean and sopping wet, than half-dried with slimy, smelly weeds and mud."

"Are you almost done preaching?" Pastor Byrd stood at the top of the stairs, a bulging garbage bag in one hand and a pile of notes in his other. "I am ready to start the cabin inspection report and see who these stuffed varmints belong to. In fact, I've *been* ready, but someone," he nodded his head toward Carly, "was up on her soapbox preaching to all of you."

"I'm done," Carly said. She bowed to Pastor Byrd and said, "You may now have the floor."

Once the laughter and hoots had settled down, Pastor Byrd looked at Carly and asked, "Since you seem intent on sending a message, would you ring the bell?"

Carly dashed over to the bell and pulled the rope, and the sound echoed over the valley. The campers who had been walking to the lodge set off at a dead run.

Cabins Four and Seven did not win the cabin clean-up. In fact, the cousins and their cabinmates ended up at the back of the line for supper. While they waited, they discussed the afternoon activities.

"What was your favorite part of Water Day, Molly?" Max asked.

"Duck, duck, splash."

"I liked the slip and slide," Carly said. "I didn't want to do the tug of war over the creek, though; I didn't want to end up in the pond again."

"The balloon slingshots were the best!" Brandon said.

"Oh, yeah!" Jess said. "I hit the archery hut once. I tried and tried to do it again, but missed."

"I almost hit it once, but then I got the bloody nose," Max said. They finally made it to the food line. "Oh, you will never guess what I heard while I was waiting for my nose to stop bleeding?"

Carly picked up a tray. "What?"

"Jeremy said the man who used to be the cook at camp is missing. He has Alzheimer's and wandered off. Mrs. Hammond spotted it on the front page of the paper when they were in town, and she got really upset. I guess Miss Gilly was upset, too."

"She still looks miserable." Carly tilted her head toward the serving window, where Miss Gilly watched to make sure the campers didn't fill up on cookies.

Miss Gilly's normally cheerful face was turned upside down. Wherever lines should go up, they now stretched down. While the children watched, she took the corner of her apron and wiped her eyes before bellowing at Peter as he picked up his cookies, "Two cookies, *only* two cookies."

Peter jumped, grabbed two cookies, and hurried away. Brandon laughed. "Boy, she scared him."

Carly waited her turn to be served. "Yum, it's chicken and baked potatoes. I'm hungry."

"Me, too," Max rubbed his stomach. "Even with those Oreos, my stomach growled half the afternoon."

Carly sighed. "I sure hope no one takes food tonight. I'm all out of candy."

Once they were seated with Slim and Aunt Susie, Carly dug right into her food. *This might be the best chicken I've ever eaten. Or maybe I'm just extra hungry tonight.*

"Will you guys patrol again tonight, Slim?" Max asked. Slim's arm stopped with his fork halfway to his mouth.

"We were awake when you left the cabin last night, remember?" Brandon said.

"It didn't work, though; someone still took food." Chad buttered a roll. "I don't think it's anyone from the camp. I think someone else sneaks in to get food. I thought maybe it was the man Corrie saw in the woods."

"We thought so, too," Max said. "But we ran into his son on our hike, and he said they're set up in the campground. Why would he come over here and steal food?"

"A guy stopped here on Tuesday asking questions," Dorie said. "I told him to go talk to Pastor Byrd, but he just turned around and left." She snapped her fingers and leaned forward. "That's who it was." She dropped her voice. "Those guys I spotted on the hill above Cabin One. One of them reminded me of someone. I'm sure it was the guy who was here Tuesday. He had an orange cap."

Slim sopped up corn juice from his plate with his roll. "Don't you kids worry about it. Pastor Hall and Pastor Byrd are on top of safety at this camp. That's one of their jobs—not the Rawson-Johnson Detectives'. Yours is to listen to the messages and have lots of fun."

Carly took another bite of chicken. *Easy for him to say. He can go get treats from Miss Gilly whenever he wants. We can't even have canteen.*

When Pastor Byrd got up to introduce the speaker for the evening service, he had a serious look on his face.

Uh-oh. Wonder if something else is missing?

"Before the evangelist comes, I have a prayer request. Carl Sherwood, better known to most of us as 'Cookie,' has wandered away from the home where he lives. He suffers from Alzheimer's, and he's been missing since early Monday morning. As you can imagine, his family and friends, which includes many of us here, are quite worried for him." He stopped as his voice cracked and waited a minute. "I would like to have the evangelist lead in prayer now, asking that Mr. Sherwood would be found soon and that he would be found safe."

After the evangelist prayed, Carly looked around. Most of the adults were wiping away tears. "If it was Miss Gilly, I'd be devastated," she whispered to Molly. "I sure hope he's all right."

When the evangelist asked everyone to bow their heads at the end of his message, Max bolted from his seat to the back of the room, fingers firmly clamped over his nose. His mom saw him coming and met him at the door to the men's bathroom. "Come into the kitchen," she whispered. "I'll get you an ice pack." Max followed her into the kitchen and glanced around to see if anyone else was there. He knew Miss Gilly liked him, but he still felt like a trespasser.

"Here, I'll hold your nose while you wash up," she said. Max washed his hands at the sink right inside the door, then took the paper towel from his mom and held his nose like she had shown him earlier. Mrs. Rawson handed him a glass of water and pointed to the table. "Sit down over there. I'll get an icepack."

Dorie came into the kitchen. "Do you need help?" She sat down at the table with Max.

"I don't think so, Dorie. We've got it covered."

Max held his nose with one hand and reached for the newspaper someone had left on the table. *Sure is weird to see a newspaper at camp. We seem so far from the outside world.* The headline caught his attention. "Elderly Man Missing from Local Nursing Home." Under the words were two pictures. Max jumped up, knocking over his chair. "MOM!" She pulled her head out of the freezer and put a finger to her lips. "These men—I've seen these men!" Dorie grabbed the paper and looked at the article. She squealed.

"This one is the man who was here on Tuesday." Her finger stabbed the picture with the smaller headline below it: "Police Wish to Speak to This Man About Mr. Sherwood's Disappearance."

"Shh!" Pastor Byrd stuck his head through the door. "What's going on in here?"

"Pastor Byrd, Pastor Byrd," Max waved the paper and hurried over to the director, Dorie right behind him. "This man." He shook the paper. "He's the one Molly and I saw on the hike yesterday. Ask her; I'm sure of it." Pastor Byrd took the paper. Max pointed to the younger man. "Then all of us on the hike saw this man. He told us Mr. Sherwood was his dad, and their name was Munster; but this article says his name is Roger Evans."

Dorie pointed to Mr. Evans. "He's the one who came by Tuesday. Remember, I told you about him?"

Pastor Byrd stared at Max and Dorie, then Mrs. Rawson. "Go get Molly and Alex out of the service."

"Bring Corrie, too," Max said. "Maybe Mr. Sherwood is the Cookie Monster she told you about."

Pastor Byrd nodded, and Mrs. Rawson hurried across the kitchen and out the door.

Less than a minute later, Mrs. Rawson was back with the others. When they looked at the pictures, there was no doubt.

"That's him," said Molly. "That's the man who told us not to get too far behind the group. And that's the man who said he was his son."

Alex nodded. "No wonder he was so nervous."

"It's the Cookie Monster," squealed Corrie.

Miss Gilly walked into the kitchen. "Gilly." Pastor Byrd put his arm over her shoulder. "These kids saw Cookie up in the woods. Can you call his daughter and get her out here? We need to call the police, too." He looked at the campers. "You kids can go to the campfire. We sure do appreciate your help."

When Max and Molly left the kitchen, the service was finished, and the others were waiting. "You will never believe what happened," Max said. "It's Cookie. The old man in the woods and the Cookie Monster Corrie saw—they're both Cookie."

"How do you know?" Carly asked.

"The picture in the paper. It was him."

"And don't forget the other guy," Dorie said. She told them how the police were looking for Roger because they thought he helped Cookie get out of the nursing home without being seen.

"But why would he do that?" Carly asked. "And why would he bring him here?"

"The treasure," Jess said. "Miss Gilly and Alex both said Cookie talked all the time about his discovery. I bet that guy wants Cookie to help him find some more."

"But how did Cookie end up here at the camp without the guy?" Brandon asked.

No one had an answer for that.

"He must be cold and hungry," Molly said as they left the lodge to go to the campfire. "Unless he's found a warm place to sleep at night and some food . . . "

"Oh! I bet—" Carly said.

"I bet he's the guy who was in the bathroom that night and took my flashlight," Jess interrupted her.

"And told the campers to be quiet the first night," Molly added.

"And rang the bell," Chad said.

"And took the food from the kitchen," Carly said, before she could be interrupted again.

Max, Jess, and Brandon grabbed each other's arms and shouted together, "And has been sleeping in Cabin One."

CHAPTER 11

"We have to tell Pastor Byrd," Max said. He dashed to the lodge, the others right behind him. They didn't even slow down when they got inside but ran full speed to the kitchen and piled through the door.

"What's going on?" Carly's dad put his hand on Max's shoulder.

"We think we know where Cookie is," Max said, his voice shaking.

"At least, he was there last night," Brandon said. "We saw a light in Cabin One last night; and when we went up there this morning to look, we found it empty, except for some candy wrappers and a flashlight that was stolen from Jess."

"And this morning, about 5:30, I woke up," Max said. "When I looked out the window, I saw someone disappear into the cabin. I think it was Cookie."

"And those two guys up above the cabin this morning," Dorie said. "I bet they were Cookie and Roger."

"Let's go look," Pastor Byrd said.

"We can't all go," said Max's mom. "We might frighten him if we all show up."

"Max, you come with us," Pastor Byrd said. "And, Gilly, you know him best. Mrs. Rawson, we might need a nurse. And Jeff." He nodded at Carly's dad. "He knows you, too."

They rushed out the back door; and when Pastor Byrd and the others headed to Cabin One, the rest stood on the porch and watched.

Max and Pastor Byrd led the way. Pastor Byrd knocked, but when there was no response, he opened the door.

"Cookie, are you in here?" Miss Gilly asked, as the door swung open.

The room was dim, dusty, silent, and empty. Cookie wasn't there.

The group stood in shocked disappointment for a moment. Then Max moved to the bedside table. He picked up an old newspaper clipping and held it up.

"It's his article," Miss Gilly said. "He was here, and he must plan to come back."

"But where is he now?" Pastor Byrd rubbed his head. "It's late in the evening, and he must be tired."

"Maybe he's at the campground with Roger," Max said, but then he shook his head. "I don't think he really was with Roger when we went on the hike. I think Roger was trying to find Cookie, and we interrupted him."

"Well, if he isn't here, I bet he's up in the woods near the cave," Gilly said. She held up the article. "He's so fixated on this. That's where he has to be."

"I'm not sure I can find it," Pastor Byrd said.

Max looked at Uncle Jeff. He shook his head. "Me neither. It's been too long."

"Alex knows where it is," Max said. "He could take us."

Pastor Byrd held his arm out to usher the others out of the cabin. "Let's go, then. We need to get up there before it's too dark to see."

Ten minutes later, the search party, armed with flashlights and a fold-up stretcher, was ready to head out of camp. Pastor Byrd asked Pastor Jeff to go with Alex, Mrs. Rawson, and the three boys—Max, Brandon, and Jess. Max ran to the cabin and grabbed sweatshirts for the three of them. When he got back, he overheard Pastor Byrd ask Miss Gilly if she wanted to go.

She shook her head. "I can't hike anymore with my bad knee, and I don't want to slow you down. I'll stay here, pray, and have a peanut butter and jelly sandwich ready for Cookie when you get him back here."

The woods were dim, much darker than during broad daylight. The sun had already gone behind the hills, and it became harder to see by the minute. Alex led the way with the boys right behind him. Max's mom and Uncle Jeff brought up the rear.

"Be careful where you step," Alex said. "It would be easy to turn your ankle up here in the dark."

Max shone his light at his feet and tried to focus on where he stepped, but his mind raced a mile a minute. *What will we find? Is Cookie okay? Has Roger found him and taken him away?*

Or worse yet, done something to him? Max's throat tightened at the thought of Cookie, confused and tired, at the mercy of a man who cared only about treasure. He stumbled but caught himself.

Brandon groaned behind him. "This is way harder than hiking during the day."

"I'm sorry," Alex said. "I know we're moving fast, but I want to get as far as we can before it's pitch dark."

"Keep going," Max said. "We'll be all right."

"We're okay back here," Uncle Jeff said. "I'll let you know if we need to stop."

Ten minutes later, Max was ready to ask for a rest stop when Alex halted and put his hand up. Max heard voices up ahead. "We're almost there," Alex whispered. "How should we proceed?" He looked at Pastor Jeff.

"Let's move closer, but be as quiet as possible. Maybe we can see what's happening before we let them know we're here."

The group crept up the trail, stepping lightly to prevent broken twigs. They pointed their flashlights straight down. Max tensed up as the voices grew louder. This wasn't a happy conversation.

Alex stopped, and the others gathered around him. They stood on the edge of a clearing and in the dim light, Max could make out the forms of Cookie and Roger Evans. Cookie sat on a rock outcrop, and Roger stood over him, shouting.

"I brought you all the way out here so we could find that treasure, and you run off and hide from me!" He shook his fist at the old man. "You know I could get in trouble for helping you leave the nursing home. Tell me where the treasure is, or you'll wish you had!"

"I told you I don't believe there is any treasure here," Cookie said, his voice quiet but firm. "I think what we found when we were kids was just something the robbers missed when they came back for it."

"I don't believe you! If you don't tell me where it is, I'll . . . "

Cookie pushed himself to his feet with the support of a walking stick and stood tall. His voice rolled out like thunder. "You'll what? I might be old, but I'm not dead!" He waved his stick at the younger man.

Roger looked like he would explode. "Why, you pathetic, old man . . . "

"Now, hold on!" Uncle Jeff stepped into the clearing and shone his flashlight in Roger's face. "I don't think you need to threaten Cookie."

Both men jumped, startled by the sudden interference. Max stepped up next to Uncle Jeff and Alex. The others crowded into the clearing behind them.

Roger looked at the group, spat out a few ugly words, and turned to run. Quick as a flash, Cookie's walking stick shot out, caught Roger's feet, and the man tumbled to the ground. He jumped up and fled into the dark. Jess started to follow, but Uncle Jeff stopped him. "Let him go, Jess. The authorities are looking for him. He won't get out of the campground."

Max's mom rushed over to Cookie. "Hi, Cookie. It's me . . . Joanna." She grabbed Uncle Jeff's arm and pulled him closer. "You remember my brother, Jeff Johnson? We used to come to camp when we were little kids, even before we could be campers."

Cookie looked at her, his eyes a bit glazed, and sat down on the stone. "Joanna and Jeff." A smile lit his face. "I remember you. You went and married those Rawson kids, didn't you?"

Pastor Jeff laughed. "We sure did. We've been worried about you! Are you all right?"

Cookie shook his head. "I don't know what's going on, but that one . . . " He shook his stick in the direction Roger had run. "That one thinks he can tell me what to do." He grimaced and pointed to his foot. "I can't walk. He knocked me down today, and I hurt it."

"I guess you're even then," Brandon said. "You sure took him down with that stick."

"Oh, yeah," Jess said. "That was awesome." Everybody laughed, and Max felt the tension drain from his body.

Pastor Jeff put his hand on Cookie's shoulder. "You are stronger than you look; but let's get down to camp, and we'll have your ankle checked out. We've got a stretcher here and some strong boys to help carry it."

Cookie looked over at Max, Brandon, and Jess. He stared hard at Max, and a confused look crossed his face. "Why, there's that Rawson boy now. The one you married." He looked at Joanna and shook his head. "But that don't make sense. I'm hungry. I need some food and sleep."

"Me, too, Cookie," Max's mom said. "Me, too. Let's go. I have it on good authority that Gilly will have a sandwich for you when we get back."

CHAPTER 12

The next morning, Carly hurried to the window into the kitchen. "Good morning, Miss Gilly. I didn't know if you would be here or not. How's Cookie?"

Miss Gilly, her face right side up again, beamed at Carly. "Oh, girly, he'll be fine. They warmed him up and gave him some fluids. His ankle is sprained, and he's still confused off and on, of course, but he's safe. I can't believe how you kids figured it all out." She shook her head, making the wiry curls bounce.

"And you!" She looked past Carly to Max, who had come up to the window for cereal. She burst through the door and gave Max a big kiss on the cheek. "You and your friends are my heroes! You go sit down. I have a surprise for you."

Max wiped his cheek on the shoulder of his shirt as he stumbled to the table where his mom and Chad sat with Aunt Susie and Slim. The rest of the cousins and Jess followed.

"I can't believe camp's almost over already," Molly said. "This week has gone faster than any other year."

Carly poured milk on her cereal. "That's because you're a camper this year, and you're busier; plus, this year has been different. We've never had a mystery at camp before."

"You can say that again!" Max rubbed his cheek where Miss Gilly had planted the kiss. He made a face, and everyone at the table laughed.

"What time did you get home from the hospital, Aunt Joanna?" Brandon asked.

"About one this morning. I'm kind of tired, but so relieved." She looked around the table. "And so proud of all of you. The doctor said if Cookie had stayed out all night, he might not have bounced back as well. By the time we left, he looked a lot more like himself and was sitting up eating a peanut butter and jelly sandwich."

"That should have clued me in." Miss Gilly appeared at the end of the table, a tray in her hands. "I should have suspected Cookie was the culprit. Everything he took was one of his favorite foods." She plopped the platter, piled with pancakes, down on their table. "Here are extra pancakes. I think you all earned it."

Jess whistled. "Wow! Thanks, Miss Gilly."

Max grinned at the cook. "Yeah. Thanks. We shouldn't get hungry before lunch!"

"Did they catch Mr. Evans?" Molly asked.

Carly's dad nodded. "They sure did. He stumbled into his camp to find the police waiting. They're looking at what charges to file against him."

Carly forked another pancake. "How did Cookie get mixed up with him, anyway?"

"Apparently, he visited Cookie's roommate, and Cookie told him the story of his great find," Aunt Joanna said. "The man convinced Cookie to go hiking with him to show him the cave."

"We aren't sure what happened next," Miss Gilly said. "But I think Cookie realized he was with the wrong crowd, so he came over here to get away from him." Miss Gilly put her hands on her hips. "If it was up to me, I would charge him with kidnapping and elder abuse." With that, she marched back to the kitchen.

"Whoa!" Jess stared after Gilly. "Remind me to stay around you guys. I would hate to be on her bad side." He waved at the pancakes. "How did you get on her good side? I mean, besides finding Cookie."

"Miss Gilly likes us because before we became campers, we were kind of kitchen help," Dorie piped up. "Have you noticed how Chad, Jeremy, and the twins wash off the tables and benches? Our parents didn't allow us to just goof off at camp. We had to help any way we could."

"That's true," Mrs. Hammond said. "I think she appreciates the fact that the young children don't cause more trouble than they're worth."

"I remember Mom told me if Jesus served His disciples, I could wash some tables to help Miss Gilly," Max said.

"Yeah," Carly said. "And the line about how we shouldn't wait to be told what to do. We should look around for ways we could help."

Max's mom looked at Uncle Jeff, and they laughed. "Sounds like we turned into Dad," Uncle Jeff said.

"No kidding." Aunt Susie shook her head. "I was about ready to look around and see if Dad had walked into the room . . . I remember both he and Mom teaching us those life lessons."

"You're lucky," Jess said. "You have a big family, and all of you are Christians. It must be easy to live right at your house."

Max shook his head. "We aren't perfect, that's for sure. I still get in trouble—mostly when Chad annoys me and we fight or I pick on Chad just to wind him up."

"Let's get moving," called Mr. Paul from the dirty dish bins. "Quit your lollygagging and get those trays up here. We don't have all day."

Chad scrambled from his seat. "Okaly dokaly, I'm done; I'll start washing tables."

"Okaly dokaly!" Max's mom said. "Where did you get that one?"

Chad's eyes twinkled. "I don't remember. But it's my new favorite. Okaly dokaly, wowee pizowwie! Okaly dokaly smokaly!" He giggled and hurried over to the dirty plate bins, repeating his new favorite phrase the entire way.

"Okaly dokaly, Chad," Molly said. "I'm right behind you." She wiped her hands on her napkin and followed Chad to the bins.

Max shook his head, then grabbed his tray. "We better hurry. We promised yesterday to be early to help clean the cabin."

"Okaly dokaly," Brandon said. "Let's go."

Max's mom dropped her head to her hands and groaned.

The day rushed by like all the others; and before they knew it, they were sitting down for the evening service. The excitement had reached a feverish pitch. This was when the overall team winner—as well as memory awards and the camper of the week awards—would be announced. Max looked across the aisle at Carly, who was chewing her nails.

He nudged Brandon. "Carly's pretty nervous. I sure hope she wins the overall memory award. She worked hard."

"She sure did. I don't know how she was able to keep her focus and memorize this week. All the mysterious happenings kept me from doing my best." Brandon pulled out his folder. "I didn't memorize as many as last year."

An hour later, the awards were all in the winners' hands. Carly did win the overall award, as well as first place for her grade level. The surprise of the evening was Jess, who won third place for his grade level. When they announced his name, Max slapped him on the back, jumped to his feet, and cheered. Jess grinned from ear to ear as he stood at the front with the other winners.

Pastor Byrd explained the Camper of the Year Award before announcing the winners. "This award is given to the boy and girl camper who have demonstrated a godly attitude throughout the week. When the other campers hear these names called, they should be able to say to themselves, 'Yes, I know why they won.' These campers aren't chosen by me, but by the counselors. So, without any further delay, I want to announce the Campers of the Year are Max Rawson and Carly Johnson."

This time, Jess was the first one up, and he whistled and clapped the loudest of all the campers. As the applause subsided, Pastor Byrd raised his hand to quiet the group.

"I have one more announcement. We have a special guest tonight who would like to make a presentation." He looked to the back of the auditorium and motioned for them to come up.

Max glanced over his shoulder. "It's Cookie, and that must be his daughter with him," Max whispered to Jess. "I can't believe he's here." As the lady rolled the wheelchair up the aisle, the name Cookie flew through the crowd; and when he reached the front, everyone stood and cheered.

"As you've figured out, this is Cookie," Pastor Byrd said when the cheering had stopped. More cheers arose, this time led by the adults in the crowd.

"We love you, Cookie," shouted Uncle Jeff.

Pastor Byrd raised his hand, and the crowd settled. "This is his daughter Sandra, and they have an announcement to make. But first, Sandra wanted me to have the young people responsible for finding Cookie come up front." When no one moved, he laughed. "Come on, Johnson and Rawson cousins, Jess, Hammond kids—come on up here."

Once they had lined up in the front, Sandra pushed her father's chair over to the podium, so he sat to the side. She walked up to the podium and stood for a moment in silence. "Dad wanted to come tonight to thank all of you for finding him." She turned to the young people who stood beside her. "You don't know how much this means to all of us. We were so frightened for him, and I believe without your help, he wouldn't be here with us today." She leaned down to Cookie. "You wanted to say something."

Cookie looked around the group, then at his daughter. "Dad, you wanted to say something to the kids who found you."

Cookie nodded and looked around the room. "Thank you very much. And thank you, Lily, my Gilly, for the peanut butter and jelly."

The campers erupted again in applause, chanting, "Gilly! Gilly! Gilly!"

Cookie picked up the word and chanted along with them, punching the air with his fist each time they said her name. Finally, Miss Gilly hurried to the front to give the old man a big hug. Then she stood between Sandra and Cookie, while Sandra continued.

"Our family would like to show our appreciation in another way. We have a check here for one thousand dollars, which we would like to be used to start the Carl 'Cookie' Sherwood Scholarship Fund. We want this money to be used to help children attend camp. This camp meant the world to our family, and Dad said he would rather have a gift given in his name while he's still alive than after he's dead." She handed the check to Pastor Byrd. The applause was deafening as the audience stood to their feet once again.

Cookie struggled to his feet, and the crowd quieted, waiting for him to balance himself on his feet. He lifted his face to the ceiling and began to sing in a strong, clear voice, "Great is thy faithfulness! great is thy faithfulness . . . "

As he sang, the crowd joined in, and the chorus of the old hymn filled the room. "Morning by morning new mercies I see."

Max looked around at the singing crowd, the old man with his face upturned toward Heaven and Jess beside him, and a wave of joy flooded over him. He joined in as they sang the end of the chorus. "All I have needed Thy hand hath provided; Great is thy faithfulness, Lord, unto me!"

THE END

Historical Resources

Oroblanco, "Lame Johnny's Treasure - Canyon Springs Stage Robbery - 45 POUNDS OF GOLD!" TreasureNet. com, http://www.treasurenet.com/forums/printthread. php?t=114861&pp=15&page=1 (accessed October 14, 2017).

Velder, Tim. "Foundation Helps Restore Historic Mallo Cabin." Powder River Energy Corporation, https://precorpfoundation. org/news-events (accessed October 14, 2017).

Others In This Series

The Double Cousins and the Mystery of the Missing Watch

The Double Cousins and the Mystery of the Torn Map

The Double Cousins and the Mystery of the Rushmore Treasure

The Double Cousins and the Mystery of Custer's Gold

The Double Cousins and the Mystery of the Russian Jewels

Also by Miriam Jones Bradley

The Nearly Twins and the Secret in the Mason Jar

All I Have Needed—A Legacy for Life

*You Ain't From Here, Are Ya? Reflections on Southern Culture
from an Outsider*

If you enjoyed this book and
would like to read more by

MIRIAM JONES BRADLEY

please visit:

www.MiriamJonesBradley.com
miriamjonesbradley@gmail.com
@AuthorMiriam
www.facebook.com/DoubleCousinsMysteries

For more information about
AMBASSADOR INTERNATIONAL
please visit:

www.ambassador-international.com
@AmbassadorIntl
www.facebook.com/AmbassadorIntl

www.ingramcontent.com/pod-product-compliance
Lightning Source LLC
Chambersburg PA
CBHW070556180626
46817CB00005B/1865